BOHEMIA CHILLS

by

Lucy Lakestone

VELVET PETAL PRESS

Florida

Published by Velvet Petal Press, Florida

Learn more about the author at LucyLakestone.com

Cover design and lightning photography by Sky Diary Productions

Couple photo by g_studio, DepositPhotos

Ebook ISBN: 978-1-943134-21-2

Paperback ISBN: 978-1-943134-20-5

First edition

ABOUT THE COMMON ELEMENTS
ROMANCE PROJECT

While *Bohemia Chills* is the seventh book in my Bohemia Beach Series of hot romances — all of which can be read on their own — it's also a Common Elements Romance Project novel. The idea of common elements intrigued me, so I couldn't resist adding one more book to my series and joining this nifty project, which features dozens of romance authors writing in a variety of subgenres.

Each of our books has to have five elements: a lightning storm, a person named Max, a stack of thick books, lost keys, and a house that may or may not be haunted. What all of these said to me was: Halloween romantic comedy! I hope the story of Kayla and Landon and their Florida town's most famous haunted house gives you the best kind of chills.

CHAPTER 1

ou don't know what it's like to be haunted by failure until you use your master's degree in film production to shoot video dating profiles.

Today's batch was a case in point. There was a guy with the personality of a turnip who told the camera he only dated blondes who talked like Marilyn Monroe.

And another one who liked "light beer and, you know, skating, dude. And gangster movies. Dude, chick flicks give me hives."

And the engineer who wanted a serious girlfriend but only if her body was "tight" and she was available Tuesdays and Thursdays, because his other nights were committed to his no-girls-allowed gaming sessions.

At least he was committed to something. Dude.

It was a job, sure. Shooting dating videos paid the rent for the apartment I shared with the most irritating man on the planet.

But really this job was my punishment for screwing up my life.

I was supposed to be telling stories with my degree — beautiful, visual stories. I couldn't coax a story out of these guys (today it was only guys, for some reason) with a book of Mad Libs and a bottle of tequila.

But props to them for getting out there. This job wasn't just a reminder of my career failures. It was a reminder of my amorous ones, too.

Because after the romantic and vocational disaster that was my first job, I was not putting myself out there, looking for love like these guys were, until I figured out what the hell my next move was.

OK, let me be honest. I was *never* putting myself out there, not after a burn so bad, smoke was still rising off my heart.

Maybe I wasn't shopping for guys, but I still wanted a new job. I'd applied for a cool video gig with the new joint Bohemia-Bohemia Beach tourism office. I hadn't heard a squeak from them after a month. Not a good sign.

So here I was, trying to make *Casablanca* out of crap.

I finished going through the standard personality questions with the guy who only dated on Tuesdays and Thursdays and handed him off to the photographer.

Just how long would this job last? More to the point, how long would I last in it? It was the brainchild of a startup jumping into the dating app market with video-heavy profiles. The concept was retro, but they gave it a twenty-first-century spin. After these studio chats with our alpha testers, we'd shoot them in the wild — the skater skateboarding, the engineer gaming, that kind of thing. The pro videos would turn the daters into mini movie stars. And, lucky me, I would get to film them.

But first, I needed to figure out the highest point on the causeway bridge so I could jump off it.

Who was I kidding? I never even jumped off the high dive during swimming lessons. Too scary.

What I needed was other options.

The clock on the wall said it was four. Good. No more appointments today.

I wandered into the bullpen, where the half-dozen coders and data people were having an end-of-shift Nerf gun war. Even the managers from the glass offices that overlooked the river were fully engaged. I ducked a foam bullet and crouched behind my desk.

"Kayla!" called Maria, our office manager. She hid behind a cushy chair in the "chill" area until she jumped up with her weapon and let fly a hail of bright yellow foam missiles. "Your damn phone has been ringing every fifteen minutes."

"Sorry. Thought it was on silent," I said as she ducked again. I couldn't bring my phone into the studio during filming, so I missed a lot of calls. Or I would if I actually got calls, which were sort of rare these days.

I opened my bottom drawer, pulled out an orange, squishy stress-relief ball with the company logo on it and hurled it at Rick, the founder and CEO. He was so busy firing little balls out of his big Rival Prometheus weapon that he didn't see it coming, and it beaned him right on the head.

"Argh!" he exclaimed.

"Yes!" Maria cheered, her brown eyes flashing in excitement.

Sensing weakness, the others turned their weapons on Rick, and he went down in a hail of bouncy ammo, effectively ending the battle for the day. I settled in my chair and dug my phone out of my backpack.

My mom.

Shit. Six calls from my mom. No messages.

I hoped they weren't about Grandma Helen. Her health was mostly good, but she was also pretty old. Mom and Grandma lived together in a bungalow in Bohemia Beach that they rented for a pittance from my Aunt Ginny and her newish husband, Jay, who lived right next door. Mom couldn't afford anything else, and it was cozy to be near family. But the little house was way too cozy for me to live there, too.

I hit the callback button.

It barely rang before she picked up. "Kayla! Honey, can you come over for dinner?"

"Uh, this is why you called me six times?"

"Well." There was an uncomfortable silence. "You can bring Landon."

My obnoxious roomie? "Why would I bring Landon?"

"He has to eat, especially after working construction all day."

"I'm sure he has other plans, Mom." And I was sure they involved a woman. He always goaded me with vague references to his endless cavalcade of dates.

"Ask him, OK?"

I sighed and rolled my eyes. "OK." My mom had this idea that Landon and I had some kind of secret crush going on, when it was more like the relationship between a cat and a dog. I tried hard to ignore him, so I guess I was the cat.

It's not that he wasn't attractive, because he was — broad-shouldered with short, dark hair, a killer smile I called the Fireworks, and the kind of twinkly brown eyes that slayed women left and right. I could see how a guy with Landon's looks could make my mom fantasize that he was some sort of handsome prince who would be perfect for her daughter.

But I didn't know why she was so eager to push me into a relationship when, to my knowledge, she hadn't had male company in years. Maybe not since she had me, and I was still waiting to find out who the Sperm Donor was. She'd been burned worse than I had.

"Six o'clock at your Aunt Ginny's house," she said.

"Wait, what? I thought you were hosting dinner."

"You know our kitchen isn't big enough for everyone, and I only want to say this once."

Uh-oh. "Say what?"

"Just be there, OK?"

It's KIND OF cool growing up in a house full of women. First it was just me and my mom in Bohemia, and then we lived with Grandma in Cocoa Beach, and then all three of us moved in with Aunt Ginny in Bohemia Beach after Ginny got divorced. My cousin Gary lived there, too — Aunt Ginny's son — but he was usually surfing or bicycling or hanging around the art lab at Bohemia High.

I worked it out so I could keep going to high school up the road in Cocoa Beach, because that's where all my friends were. But at the end of every day, there was this welcoming nest of love and understanding at the huge beach house that fooled me into thinking the world was a nice place where I could actually realize my dreams.

Ha.

Now the beach house was owned by the Bohemia School of Art and Design, and Ginny was married to Jay, a kind accountant she'd met through her work with the art museum. He gave her the respect and love her shitty, cheating ex didn't. Aunt Ginny and Jay had a pretty, new house in Bohemia Beach that had been built on one of the few vacant lots left in a neighborhood that dated from the 1960s, and Mom rented their charmingly dated bungalow next door.

The driveway at Aunt Ginny's was full of cars under the palm trees, so I parked my seasoned sedan at Mom's house and strolled over to the modern pile of cream-white stucco with the light green metal roof, wondering what Mom wanted to talk about.

"Oh, shit." Next to Gary's beater van was a pickup truck I

knew well, loaded with ladders and tools and stuff, the Putter Homes logo on the side. It showed a guy wearing a hard hat, golfing with a hammer.

Landon.

My mom had done an end-run around me. I was fully prepared with a story about Landon being too busy to come. Truth was, I'd called him — at his office number, where I knew he wouldn't be — so I could say I tried.

OK, I was a bad person. A failure *and* a bad person.

But I shouldn't have to put up with my roommate outside of time actually spent at my Bohemia apartment, especially when sharing the rent with Landon was a symbol of just how far I'd let my life slide in the past year.

I knocked at the door for form's sake and then pushed it open to the cacophony that was my family. Their noise level had gone up a notch since Gary had gotten involved with Ez Falcon, a songwriter who played wicked piano with a rock band, Ez and the Emeralds. At least it was good noise, though the music coming from the living room seemed to bounce off the tiled floors and ricochet around the cathedral ceilings.

I wandered into the room, which had comfortable, modern furniture and big, bright art on the walls. Ez was wailing on the keys to "Come Sail Away," the old Styx power ballad, her short, dark hair flopping around, and Gary was playing — bongos? He was a potter most of the time and did some foam sculpting on fancy trim work on McMansions, but he also had a thing for music, especially drums. And he was the nicest guy around.

Gary and Ez belted out the lyrics, and to my surprise, Jay played along on electric guitar. Or maybe I should say he just tried to keep up. The overhead lights glinted off the silver in his brown hair.

Grandma, a bony spark plug with a white-haired pixie cut, sat on the couch with her two redheaded daughters, my mom and Aunt Ginny. Grandma banged her cane on the floor to the beat as Ginny played a tambourine and Mom rapped a cowbell with a drumstick, all of them grinning.

Leaning against an open doorway on the other side of the room, arms crossed in a way that showed off every muscle under his white T-shirt, was Landon. He smiled and nodded along to the song. He was the first to notice me, and that's when he blasted me with the full Fireworks, enhanced by dimples and deliciously formed lips surrounded by just the faintest hint of scruff. No wonder women fell all over him.

I mean, not that I'd been paying that much attention.

He nodded at me, then nodded toward the musicians.

I shook my head. He'd witnessed my drunken banjo playing once. Now he asked me every chance he got whether I'd been to the holler lately.

I'm from the swamp, thank you very much, like everybody else who grew up in Florida. *Not* the holler.

And he grew up in a big house on a golf course, in a development created by his dad. To me, that's a step down from a holler or a swamp. At least hollers and swamps still have remnants of nature and don't suck all the water out of the aquifer.

Sorry. I get a little worried about the water sometimes.

The song came to its pounding conclusion, and everyone clapped and laughed.

"Kayla!" Gary called. "Did you bring your banjo?"

"Nope," I said, then shot a glower at Landon. As if he'd psychically planted the idea in Gary's head.

"Too bad," said Ez, whose moods had lightened since she'd taken up with Gary. She smiled up at him from the piano bench, then grabbed a handful of his curly hair and pulled him toward her for a kiss.

My heart squeezed for just a second. I'd never have that, that *thing* they had. I was stupid to even think I should try. I'd been even more stupid not to foresee how my bad judgment would crash my career before it even got started.

"I have to interrupt the music anyway," Aunt Ginny said. "Gary's going to grill the burgers for me."

"Oh, that's right! Sorry, Mom," he said, and he dashed off to the kitchen, followed by his mother and Jay.

Ez shrugged. "I'll play background music, then. Carry on." Her fingers floated over the keys, coaxing out one of those melancholy ballads she was so good at writing.

Mom stood, patting Grandma's shoulder so she wouldn't feel obligated to get up, then came over to me and gave me a hug. "I'm glad you're here. And it's so nice Landon could come."

I wanted to ask, *Why do you care if Landon is here?* But I just smiled at her and asked, "What did you want to tell me?"

A little wrinkle of concern appeared in her brow for a moment. "It's nothing to worry about. I'll tell everyone over dessert."

"Are you sick? Is something wrong?"

"Nothing's wrong, sweetie." She smoothed back her red hair, her tell. I knew she was anxious about something.

"Don't make me worry all through dinner."

"I promise it's nothing to worry about. OK?"

"OK." My tone was dubious at best, but she just gave me another quick hug and headed to the kitchen.

"Thanks for inviting me to dinner."

I whirled at the voice behind me. It was Landon, of course, and now his smile was full of mischief.

I swallowed. "I — I called your office."

"You know the office closes at four."

"If I'd tried to call your cell, you wouldn't have been able to hear it over the mating cries of the hoochies at whatever happy hour you usually frequent."

He slapped a hand to his chest and made an expression of

pain. "You wound me. Is that what you think of me? And do you see me at happy hour? No, I'm here, about to enjoy a delicious family dinner."

"Because my mother invited you."

"She might've called. And she didn't even have to shout over hoochie mating cries to be heard."

Now my face heated a little. Was I projecting a little when it came to Landon? Maybe not every guy was as crappy as my former boss. But then again, Landon seemed to be on the bar circuit a lot, even if he never brought his conquests home to the apartment.

"Sorry," I mumbled, looking down at my chunky black Skechers. When I looked up, his smirk had softened.

"What's up?" he asked.

"I don't know," I admitted. "Mom has some kind of surprise announcement. She won't tell me what it is."

"If she told you, it wouldn't be a surprise." Now the twinkle was back.

"Oh, shut up."

"Yeah, shut up," Ez called from across the room. "I'm making art here."

CHAPTER 2

*T*he burgers were accompanied by Aunt Ginny's homemade potato salad, grilled corn on the cob, my mom's fruit salad — heavy on chunks of watermelon — and wilted spinach with garlic and butter. I didn't care if I'd be breathing garlic fire later. I was crazy about spinach and garlic and plus, I needed my vitamins, especially since I was more of a forager than a cook. I dug in like Popeye and tried not to think about whatever Mom was going to tell us.

She'd made the dessert. Another bad sign. She always baked as therapy. Only this wasn't exactly baked.

"Johanna made her famous Oreo cookie ice cream dessert, so I hope you left some room," Aunt Ginny said as she got up from the dining-room table and headed to the kitchen.

"I'll help you dish it up," Mom said, and my dread kicked up a notch. "Just stay there, Kayla, and entertain our guests," she added as I stood, ready to give them a hand.

"I'll get the coffee," Jay volunteered, following them.

"Nice art," Landon said as I retook my seat.

"What?"

My mom's empty seat was at the end of the table, next to

mine. Landon and I were seated across from Gary and Ez. Ez was chatting with Grandma at the other end, explaining exotic musical instruments made by the company she worked for.

"Nice art," Landon repeated. "The paintings. Originals, right?" He gestured to the walls of the light and airy dining room, which had a large window that showcased the golden-hour sunlight and helped illuminate the colorful canvases that hung around us.

"Mom's been collecting for years," said Gary from across the table, since I was too deep in my thoughts to respond properly. "She's always had an eye. Especially for picking up artists before they get famous."

"And expensive," Landon said.

Gary chuckled. "That too."

"Hey, I've got some work for you on a project we're doing on Merritt Island," Landon said to Gary. "Big riverfront house. They want to gild the lily with some architectural foam. Fancy window trim."

"Awesome. The art school never pays enough."

"But you're selling more of your ceramic work now, right?" I asked my cousin.

Gary smiled. "Yeah, it's starting to pick up," he said modestly. "I'm in a few galleries around town now, and I've scheduled a show in Miami."

"Fantastic!" I said. Everyone knew Gary was a potter prodigy.

"As long as you have time for me, man," Landon said. "They'll pay well. I make it clear they're getting the best."

"Thanks," Gary said.

I looked at Landon again in puzzlement. He was being so *nice.*

My roomie noticed. "What?"

"Never mind."

Jay came in with a coffeepot and started filling our cups,

followed by my mom and Aunt Ginny carrying trays of bowls stuffed with the decadent ice-cream dessert. I knew all about it because I'd watched Mom make it dozens of times. It had crushed Oreos drizzled with melted butter, vanilla ice cream, a caramel layer, whipped cream and nuts. If I had to rank the tastiest things in the world, this stuff would come a close second to Mr. Darcy in *Pride and Prejudice.*

But just when we had our first heavenly mouthfuls, my mom — who wasn't eating her dessert, I noticed — cleared her throat.

The chatter and appreciative *mmmm* sounds ceased.

"It's OK, Aunt Johanna," Gary said, seeing her discomfiture.

"Whatever it is, we're behind you a hundred percent," Ginny said.

There were murmurs of support around the table, and I relaxed just a fraction. It was good to know everyone had her back. Our backs.

"Thanks, everyone," Mom said. "I didn't mean to get you all worried. There's nothing wrong with me. Everything's fine, really. What I have to say concerns Kayla most of all."

"What?" I sat up straighter and dropped my spoon onto the table with a clatter. My vocabulary was extremely limited this evening.

"Honey," she said, turning to me, "I wanted to do this in front of everyone here so you know that we're all here if you need us."

"What is it?" OK. Vocabulary getting slightly larger.

"I've heard from lawyers representing your father," she said.

Her words seemed to echo in the room. *Your father.* "You've got to be kidding me. The Sperm Donor?"

Ez sputtered. Gary was also trying not to laugh. I could appreciate their amusement. My mother bringing up my father after my twenty-five years of blissful ignorance couldn't get any more absurd.

"What does he want?" I continued. "It's a little late to sue for custody, and I don't want anything from him."

"Currently, he doesn't want anything," my mom said dryly. "He's dead."

Oh. *Oh.*

Ez's sniggering noticeably stopped.

"And you don't really have any choice about him giving you something, because he already has, in his will."

"Wait a minute. Wait a minute." I stood. "Who *is* this guy?"

"Take it easy, honey," Mom said.

An unexpectedly kind voice penetrated my confusion. "It'll be OK, Kayla."

Landon had stood next to me and spoke in my ear. He slipped an arm around my shoulders and eased me back into my seat. There was something warm and steady about him that calmed my pounding heart. Then something hot and electric suffused me that I really shouldn't be feeling at all with my roomie, whose specialties included leaving empty beer cans on the kitchen counter and wet towels in the living room.

My mother's face had a touch of pity about it as she gazed at me with those big, blue eyes. "He is — *was* Maximillian Kantera."

"Holy shit," Landon breathed next to me.

"Max Kantera?" Jay exclaimed. "Isn't he on the art museum board?"

My Aunt Ginny nodded. *"Was."*

"And one of the biggest developers in Bohemia," Landon added.

"Does he — is he — ?" I had so many questions, and from the look on my mom's face when she saw my hurt and confusion, I wondered if she had regrets about making this announcement to the whole gang.

"His family lives in Bohemia," she said. "He's married — no, he wasn't when we met, but he'd been engaged to a society girl and didn't tell me. He has three kids. And you. Four kids."

"Not that I count." I hated to be bitter, but I'd had years of practice.

"You count, sweetheart. I think maybe he had an idea that he'd try to do one thing to make things right. I had no idea, of course."

"Well, what?" I asked. "What did he do?"

She sighed. "He left you Milkweed Mansion."

There were a few gasps around the room, but I didn't understand why until Ez squeaked out, "The goddamn *haunted house?*"

CHAPTER 3

*S*omeone suggested we take our bowls of dessert and coffees into the living room, and in that more relaxed atmosphere, I was able to sit in a corner of the couch, eat my ice cream and process the news while everyone else chatted about Milkweed Mansion.

"So supposedly a woman died in there," Ez said. "An unhappy wife killed herself."

"I heard she was axed by her husband. As in literally," Gary added.

"*Gary,*" Aunt Ginny admonished.

"Sorry," he said sheepishly.

"I thought it was a young woman who died," Ginny added in a more sensitive tone. "Poor thing."

"Poor thing what?" I asked. "Does anyone really know what happened there?"

"I knew the last family who lived there," Grandma said. "I went to school with their daughter in the early 1960s before they moved away and sold the property. She said there were always strange noises, but she didn't think the ghost was malevolent. She said she didn't know who it was."

"So there *is* a ghost?" I was skeptical, but this wasn't good news. "Great."

Somehow Landon had ended up next to me again, and because my mom and my skinny grandma were crammed onto the couch with us, his jeans-clad thigh was snug against mine. His proximity was making me toasty. Or maybe it was because it was still summerlike in mid-September in Bohemia Beach. Summer didn't really end here till late November.

But the AC was cranked, and the air was cool. It was my stupid roommate who was hot.

"When I was a kid, my brothers and I used to climb over the fence, sneak around the back of the house and try to listen for the ghost," Landon said. "Usually we just ended up with a bunch of sand spurs stuck to our clothes and to our dog Creampuff. A big golden. It took hours to get them all out."

I shot him a look of disbelief. "Your dog was named Creampuff?"

"Blame my mom," Landon said. "She's the baker."

"That property has to be worth something," said Jay, ever the accountant. "It's right there in Bohemia's historic district on a bend in the river road, on a big lot full of mature oak trees. It overlooks the lagoon on a kind of cliff. Fantastic views."

"Yeah, but have you seen the house lately?" Landon said. "It looks like 1313 Mockingbird Lane."

"*The Munsters,*" I moaned. "I've inherited the house from *The Munsters.*"

Landon laughed. "Only the Munsters' house was in better shape."

"I guess you could knock it down," Jay said.

"No!" the Fetheroles chorused. The Fetheroles being Grandma, Mom and Aunt Ginny (who was a Fetherole before she became a Gorski and then an unexciting Jones).

I was a Fetherole, but I didn't chorus. "Why not?" I asked.

"It's *historic*," Aunt Ginny said.

"OK, OK." I liked historic houses too, but I was also broke. "Is it on a national register or something?"

"No," said Landon. "I don't think anyone ever cared enough to make that happen."

I huffed, making my light-brown bangs flutter. "And why not? Why the hell did the Sperm Donor" — Ez snickered again — "buy that house and just leave it neglected for — how long did he own it, anyway?"

"I think he had it for about twenty years," Mom said. "That's what the property records say. And I don't know why he neglected it."

"He invested in a lot of properties, not all of them well-maintained," Landon said. "When my dad wanted to develop any choice piece of land on the west side of town, half the time he had to go through Max Kantera."

I rolled my eyes. "And why didn't he leave it to his real kids?"

Gary shot me a look that was a mix of encouragement and pity. "You're real."

"Are we sure?" Landon pinched my arm.

I jumped. "Hey!"

"See?" he said as the others laughed. "Definitely real."

This was why he was annoying. Though those crinkles around his eyes when he laughed were kind of cute.

"Well," Jay said. "Maybe I shouldn't say — "

"What?" I asked.

"Sometimes people will leave someone something so one heir doesn't sue the estate with a claim for more. By citing you specifically in the will, he made it clear he knew of you and thought of you and was clear about his intentions."

"So he left me a haunted house so he wouldn't have to leave me anything else? What a *fucking great guy*," I bit out.

There was an uncomfortable silence.

"I don't know his reasons," my mom said, her eyes a little watery now. "The property is beautiful and probably valuable, so I'd like to think he really did want you to have a legacy that meant something. Kayla, sweetie, you are as real and important to me as any person on this earth."

Landon got up, pushed me toward the middle of the couch so I was next to my mom, and sat on the other side of me. I gave in to my mom's hug and tried not to cry. It wasn't her fault my father was an asshole.

When I'd recovered and the hug ended, Ez moved to the piano and started playing while we kept talking.

I still had a lot of questions. "Since I didn't go to high school here, I don't know the kids — my half-siblings. I can't believe I'm saying that. Anyone know them? Gary?"

"They were all in school behind me. Andy's the younger one. Good guy," Gary said. "He works at the space center now. The other two are fraternal twins, and you've never seen twins more different. Annabel is pretty cool. She's still around, working for the family business. Max Junior is a tool."

"Chip off the old block?" I asked.

"Maybe," Gary said. "He ran with a loud, obnoxious crowd. Studied PR but was second-in-command for a while at his dad's company."

My undergraduate degree was in marketing, so we had that in common. "What does he do now?"

"Last I heard," Landon said, "Max Junior had been pushed out of the developer business and was looking for a job. I had a little contact with him when my dad's company worked with Max Senior. He was less than honest and sloppy with the details. He did everything he could to keep his sister from taking his place, but she's been second-in-command for a while now and will probably make the company that much better now that her father's gone."

Her father. *My* father. My father, the Sperm Donor Developer Haunted House Proprietor.

Did I look like him? I didn't get my mom's red hair or freckles. My longish hair was light brown with hints of gold, and my eyes were hazel, not blue like hers. Though Gary had hazel eyes, so maybe those did run in the family. My real family, the Fetheroles.

My brain was still a jumble, but just hanging out and talking with these dear people actually had made the news a little more bearable.

"So what's next?" I asked.

"Your father specified that he wanted the lawyers to tell me first about the house, so that I could tell you," my mom said. "Now that you know, you can pick up the keys to the house anytime you like."

"Yeah, but what am I going to do with a crumbling haunted house?"

"I can take a look at it with you, if you want," Landon said. "I have tomorrow afternoon off."

I turned around to look at him. "Why would you do that?"

"I build things," he said, his velvet-brown eyes twinkling again. "I might come in handy. And I've always wanted to see a ghost. It'll be fun."

Fun? He had a funny idea of fun. But I didn't want to visit a haunted house by myself, even if it was *my* house.

I nodded slowly, wondering who this generous guy was and what he'd done with my roommate. "You'd better bring a hammer. A big one."

"All my tools are of more than adequate size," he said, just loud enough that I could hear.

The corner of my mouth turned up of its own accord before I could quash my smile. I was struck with the idea that if anyone could make visiting a haunted house fun, it might be Landon.

CHAPTER 4

Milkweed Mansion was aptly named. I kind of liked the milkweed, with its orbiting butterflies. This place was butterfly heaven, with lots of wildflowers and thorny bushes in the scant sunny patches between the oaks and palms around the house.

I learned from the lawyer this morning that the nickname emerged after the property was essentially abandoned in 1962 and began its slow downfall in the hands of neglectful absentee owners, including the Sperm Donor, who picked it up for a song. Apparently ghost stories are not good for property values.

The once-grand mansion overlooked the Indian River Lagoon, which locals simply called the river. The wide stretch of sparkling water separated mainland Bohemia, where I lived now, from Bohemia Beach, where I spent my formative years.

The knotty old live oaks drooped over the weathered, rambling, two-story-plus Victorian as if they were protecting it from outsiders. The white paint on the clapboard siding was weathered and chipped with age, though an excess of faded gingerbread trim painted blue and light green held the promise of beauty.

The cone-shaped roof over a rounded section of porch on the southeast corner had damage to its tin shingles, probably from a long-ago hurricane. A tower on the next corner looked like a great place to lock up a madman. And an eclectic collection of weathervanes seemed to adorn every peak of the roof.

A decaying gazebo near the river edge of the property overlooked the lagoon with an air of shabby elegance, evoking garden parties and weddings. Surrounding the expansive, overgrown lot was a rusting, black, wrought-iron fence, and the metal gates didn't look like they'd keep out a determined raccoon. The effect was one of stately gloom.

Landon had insisted on driving us over in his pickup truck — in case he needed any of those tools, he said with the faintest quirk of the mouth — and I'd reluctantly agreed. It was Friday, late morning, and I'd taken the day off. He said he'd finished his work earlier, though I learned as we chatted on the way over that he seemed to work weekends and odd evenings, too, whenever he was on a construction project that was behind deadline. He said he often supervised crews or dealt directly with clients but jumped in and did the hard work when necessary. So maybe he wasn't partying all the time after all.

"And there's all that networking on the golf course," I remarked as we regarded the shiny chain and padlock on the gate. The lawyer hadn't given me a key for the padlock.

"I hate golf." Landon yanked on the chain. Solid.

"How can that be true?" I'd often seen him toting his clubs back and forth from the apartment. "And how can you hate golf with a name like Landon Putter?"

"Naming is destiny, I guess. My dad has stuffed golf down my throat my whole life. He says meetings are always better on the fairway." Rocking jeans and a sinfully tight black T-shirt with a cartoon of a cute sea cow that said "My Patronus Is a Manatee," Landon walked the few steps to the truck. He dug around in the back and emerged with bolt cutters. "He golfs every free minute. He watches it on TV. Even the office decor is pictures of famous golf courses. I keep telling him to buy some freakin' art."

I laughed. "Yeah, I know plenty of artists who could use the money."

Landon clamped the tool on the fat links of the gate chain, breaking it apart. He unthreaded the links from the bars of the double swing gate and pushed it open. One side of the heavy gate creaked at the unexpected pressure and fell completely off, rusty hinges shattering. We both jumped back to save our toes from destruction as it clattered to the brick driveway. .

"Cha-ching," I said, noting the first necessary repair in the small spiral notebook I was carrying.

"Let's just hope your key works on the house."

Weeds brushed at our jeans as we walked slowly up the drive to the front. I spotted a few empty beer cans and some trash amid the bushes, but it wasn't as bad as it might've been. For instance, there weren't any dead bodies.

Yet.

The porch wrapped around so far, I couldn't see where it stopped. It crept around the west side of the house, ran straight along the front on the south side, then popped out in a big hexagon before continuing around to the east, where it faced the Indian River Lagoon. I could imagine folks a hundred years ago sitting out here on their wicker chairs, enjoying a pitcher of lemonade while sweating buckets under heavy skirts and suits and smacking at squadrons of mosquitoes.

OK, maybe it wasn't so romantic after all.

Now it would be nigh impossible to relax on the porch, as we found when we climbed up the front steps. A few of the floorboards were rotten or nonexistent, like missing teeth, and the rest yowled underfoot like pissed-off cats.

"Cha-ching." Another line in the notebook.

Avoiding the obvious holes, we made it to the door. It had been pretty once. It was carved and weathered, hinting at multiple layers of paint, and plywood was nailed over the middle of it, just like most of the lower-floor windows.

"What do you make of that?" I asked Landon.

"Covering up a hole?" he mused. "Maybe a window."

"A window? Broken, no doubt."

"Probably. Nice lock, though. Brass. Ready to try it?"

"Why not?" I pulled out the key, already attached to my silver sugar-skull keychain. "It can't get much worse."

I inserted the key in the lock, and after a little jiggling, it turned. I pushed the door. It creaked open.

It got worse.

"Cha-ching, cha-ching, cha-ching," Landon remarked idly.

"Shut up," I said, but he was right.

Besides the dirt — grunge, cobwebs, bits of broken wood and tile in odd piles — there were countless indications of decay. The wood floors probably would be beautiful with tons of work, but the curving staircase that climbed up from the foyer in two flights was almost as gap-toothed as the porch. Chunks of plaster were missing from the walls, revealing slats of old wood beneath. Where there was paint, it was crackled like one of Gary's raku vases. The prisms on the chandelier above the entry hall were so encrusted with dust, they looked gray, and it was hard to tell how much of the fixture was actually there under the cobwebs.

The adjacent front parlor to the left had a fireplace with a pretty wooden mantel that badly needed a paint job. The front and interior of the fireplace were faced with tiles, though only a handful of them were left, and only one or two of those weren't broken. The fireplace actually opened to the room beyond, so we went through the connecting door to check it out.

"This is huge!" I said.

"Ballroom?" Landon mused.

Maybe it could hold fifty or sixty people. "A modest ballroom, but a much bigger room than I expected. Check out the double doors into the hallway."

"And the big windows and the designs on the parquet floors. At least these are in pretty good shape."

I peered at the ceiling. "Is that crown molding hand-carved? Wow."

"Too bad the light fixtures are missing." He gestured to the hanging wires in two places on the ceiling. "They were probably chandeliers."

"Cha-ching," I said resignedly, writing *Ballroom lights* in my notebook.

In the kitchen, mint walls hinted at better times. The good news was that the cabinets and sink had gotten an update — in, say, 1955. Which would be cool if everything wasn't so derelict.

"Let's go upstairs," Landon said, breaking the dismal silence as we stared at the scruffy cabinets, chipped sink, peeling paint and the black and white hexagonal tiles on the floor. Actually, the tiles looked pretty good, or would after a day or two of scrubbing.

"We haven't finished the downstairs yet," I said.

"We'll get there. I want to see if the floors look sound up there."

I raised an eyebrow. "By walking on them?"

He shrugged and smiled. "Carefully, yes. Besides, you don't want them falling on our head, do you?"

"I don't know," I said, looking up at the grubby tin ceiling. "Maybe it would be better if the whole thing just collapsed into a pile. We could have a bonfire and be done with it."

"That's no way to talk about a historic treasure," he said as we moved back to the foyer and began a trepidatious ascent of the staircase.

"This is pretty." I nodded at the round window on the landing, leaded in a floral design with clear, beveled panels that looked out over the porch roof and the yard. It was cruddy but miraculously intact. Buoyed, I took a few steps up the next flight with more confidence. Until I teetered on a last-minute correction to avoid putting my foot through a hole.

"Watch it!" Landon clutched my elbow as I tried to recover.

"I'm OK," I said, yanking my elbow away. The move threw me off balance, and I fell against the railing, which groaned and shifted. "Shit!"

And then I was falling.

Landon grabbed me by the arm as the section of railing crashed to the floor below us. He yanked me close, holding me tight for a second, then lifted me by the waist to a more sound step as if I was no lighter than a feather.

Trust me. I was as heavy as at least three or four feathers.

"Damn it!" Landon scowled. "Why are you so stubborn?"

"I'm not." I totally was, and scared shitless to boot. I wasn't sure what left me more breathless, near-death or the feel of Landon's muscled arms pulling me to safety. His touch launched a bolt of lightning right to all my tingly bits. "Thanks," I finally managed as I regained my cool and my breath at the top of the stairs, where the floor seemed solid enough.

"Don't mention it," Landon said, though there was an edge to his voice.

We'd reached an overlook with a limited view of the foyer. Hallways extended at forty-five-degree angles from here, each adorned with peeling wallpaper and dark sconces. As I took a few steps and peered down one of the dark corridors, there was a mighty creak behind me.

"Heavy-footed much?" I teased Landon.

"Uh, Kayla?"

His odd tone prompted me to turn toward him.

He hadn't moved an inch. "That wasn't me."

As if it were listening, the whole house seemed to sigh as the creak turned into more of a groan, underscored by a strange tinkling sound that brought to mind malevolent fairies. The maelstrom of eerie sounds shot shivers up my spine. And was that a flickering light that caught the corner of my eye as I whipped my head around, looking for the source?

Shaken, I locked onto Landon's puzzled gaze and tried not to look as creeped out as I felt. "What the *fuck* was that?"

"If I were to guess, I'd say it's a ghost. Or the house is about to fall down." He might have been joking, but it was hard to tell. "Only way to be sure is to keep looking."

CHAPTER 5

The bedrooms were as expected — kind of a mess, but at least with salvageable wooden floors. There were five on this corridor, mostly empty, but one still contained a small bed with a brass frame coated in scratched-up white paint. A child's bed?

Half a dozen horror movies leapt to mind. The door to this room had a hole in it. The bed held a tattered boxspring, and what looked like rodent droppings were on the floor under it. I tried not to think about them too hard as I mumbled "Cha-ching" and wrote down *Exterminator* in my notebook.

There was one bathroom off this hall that probably last saw a renovation around the same time as the kitchen, with pink and black tiles everywhere and a broken mirror.

"Kitschy," Landon said. "I like it."

"Really? I figured you'd like it with glass tile, faux-bronze fixtures and a waterfall shower."

"Why, Kayla — are you thinking about what I like in the shower?"

"No!" My face grew warm as we headed toward the other hallway. But now that he'd planted the image of that tautly muscled body under a cascade of pounding water — *holy shit.* "It's just that you guys build those Tuscan-tropical McMansions ... "

"My father does. I mean, I help, but it's not what I want to be doing."

"It's not?" We stepped into the one large bedroom off the second hallway — the master, I guessed, since it was a princely size, with French doors to a neat little riverfront balcony — then we briefly glanced into the funky turquoise and white bathroom there. "If you're not happy, then why are you building Hummer houses?" I asked.

"I like what I do," he said, "but I'd rather revive old homes or create retro homes in historic neighborhoods with a nod to the past. Energy-efficient and hurricane resistant. One-of-a-kind projects. Renovating really turns me on. Fixing up something like this would be a blast."

I eyed him skeptically. "You're on drugs." We exited the master bedroom suite and reached a closed wooden door at the end of the hall.

"More of a whiskey guy, actually." He grinned as he reached out and turned the knob. He had to give it a good yank before the door yawned open with a dusty sigh.

The hinges expelled a shriek as the door swung toward us, and I jumped back. The unnerving sound reminded me of the house's previous tantrum, and I looked around suspiciously before advancing toward the dimly lit space beyond. Lit by what, I wasn't sure. An enclosed spiral staircase turned up and disappeared above.

"The turret," Landon said with interest. "After you?"

"Yeah. Right." I guess it was better if I went first. Maybe he'd catch me if I fell again. "I ain't afraid of no ghosts."

"I love that movie." Landon produced a small, bright flashlight to light our way as I began the spiral climb. Maybe these dark wooden stairs were in better shape because they'd been secured behind the tight door, but they felt solid under my feet and looked decent enough. The curving white walls were a little claustrophobic, even though the stairs were wide.

The light quickly grew brighter as we climbed, and in one turn of the screw, we'd reached the top — a faceted hexagonal room about twelve feet across with five large vertical rectangular windows, each with a top panel in patterned stained glass in pretty blues and greens, like the flash in a peacock's tail.

I turned slowly and took it all in. It needed paint, and the floor could use a refinish, but ... "Good golly, this is beautiful."

"Then you're going to love this," said Landon, who'd moved to one of the windows and was looking out.

I followed, then clutched Landon's arm in excitement. "The river!"

"Spectacular, isn't it?"

Beyond the weedy lawn and gnarly old oaks and palms, over the short cliff that edged the property, the Indian River Lagoon sparkled. Today the water was a steely blue-gray with glints of diamonds as it stretched north and south as far as the eye could see. And straight ahead, to the east, was the narrow green barrier island that held Bohemia Beach, dotted with seemingly tiny houses and docks on the far side of the river. The taller hotels and condos and a strip of blue ocean were just visible at the horizon beyond.

"OK, this is pretty sweet." I self-consciously released Landon's arm, even though my hand was kind of enjoying itself. "This would make a great studio."

"A writer's garret?"

"Painter's. Photographer's. You could do definitely do photo shoots here."

"Or board meetings," Landon said.

I looked at him aghast to catch him grinning again. I shook

my head. "Geez, I thought you were serious. Anyway, it's not big enough. Unless you have a really small board."

"My board is plenty big," he said, and I smacked his arm. He laughed, but he didn't move away. His body was just touching mine as we stood side by side, taking in the small boats on the river and the clouds dotting the blue sky. All of a sudden the light and airy — OK, musty, but airy — space seemed a lot smaller.

"Maybe it could be an observatory?" I asked softly, trying not to notice his heady cedar-lime soap scent and the way the hairs on his arm were igniting gooseflesh on mine. He was taking up all the air in the airy room.

"Or a bedroom," he whispered, and when I looked up, he was staring at me intently, with none of his usual glib humor. Those lips, usually smiling, were instead serious. Can lips be serious? They looked serious, and moist, and slightly open as if he were struggling for breath. And his dark eyes held mysteries and depths I had no idea he was capable of.

I swallowed, tore myself from his magnetic pull and took a step back. "Yeah, well, it's a long way down if you have to go to the bathroom in the middle of the night."

Landon blinked, then a corner of his mouth turned up. "All you need is a chamber pot."

"Gross."

"Or a chute?"

I groaned and laughed at the same time. Nothing like potty humor to make me forget — almost — that he was hotter than a lava flow in July. "Now that you mentioned a bathroom, maybe we should wrap this up. I'm remembering all that coffee I had this morning."

"Agreed. Let's finish the tour. But at least you know you have one good room."

"If I can only get to it without falling on my ass."

"Right." He gestured to the steps. "After you. And be careful."

We reached the second-floor hallway below without incident, and he peered around a rounded wall into a corner I hadn't even noticed was there.

"What is it?" I asked.

"Another door?" He opened it. "Another staircase under the top one. Back stairs. Not uncommon in a house like this."

"If it's better than the others, I'm all over it."

"It's not a spiral, and it looks solid. But let me go first this time, just in case." He brought out the small flashlight again, though a window on a landing halfway down made it mostly unnecessary.

Two flights brought us down behind the kitchen. Better yet, the stairs were actually intact, though the one just above the landing sounded like a dying frog when we stepped on it. I might have jumped a little.

We gave what appeared to be a very roomy dining room a quick glance — it had a great river view but was as dilapidated as everything else — and moved toward the other room at the back of the house.

"This is the last one, right?" I asked.

"Yep." The ornate wooden door was closed. Landon tried the knob. "It's locked."

My eyebrows popped up. "Why would it be locked?"

"Monsters?" Landon suggested. "Meth lab? Did the lawyer give you any other keys?"

"Just the one."

"Might as well try it."

I shook my head, doubting it would work. I jiggled the key and turned the knob. "I think something clicked, maybe? But it won't open."

"Let me try." Landon turned the key and knob as I had, but he also leaned heavily on the door.

The seal popped and the door swung in so fast, it brought Landon with it. He landed hard on his side in the darkened room as a musty miasma surrounded us.

"Are you OK?" I squealed, kneeling next to him, not sure whether to touch him. An angel and a demon had a rapid-fire argument inside my head about the pros and cons of touching Landon.

"Fine. All in a day's work." He sounded grumpy, but he gave me a half smile and held out a hand. I grabbed it, stood, and made a show of pulling him to his feet.

It was pretty nice touching Landon.

Only then did I look around. I sucked in a breath. "Is this what I think it is?"

CHAPTER 6

*L*andon, still dusting himself off, moved to where speckles of light were shining through tall curtains on one side of the room. He tugged at the drapes, and in slow motion, they disintegrated off their curtain rods, leaving behind a tornado of dust motes swirling in a wash of sun. The sudden illumination revealed a time capsule: a dazzling library.

A *dusty* dazzling library, to be sure. Still, it was just the sort of thing I'd always hoped a library would be when I escaped into books as a kid. For one thing, it had splendid light, and the top panels of the large windows were blue and green stained glass, like what we'd seen in the turret. At the back of the house, this room faced north into what was probably a lovely garden at one time. Now the view was mostly trees and scrubby bushes.

I hugged myself at the discovery of this unexpected treasure. "This is incredible. Last night online I read that the original owner, Mrs. Fountain, started Bohemia's first library."

"She must have loved books," Landon said. "And no one else cared enough to take them out of here."

Floor-to-ceiling bookcases were stuffed with volumes, their spines a rainbow of muted colors, promising adventure and ancient knowledge. A rolling ladder allowed access to the top shelves. Resting in a round wooden stand was a globe that was probably outdated fifty times over. Big shapes in the middle of the room were covered with fabric that once was white.

"I hope those books don't disintegrate like the curtains did," I said.

"Valid concern." Landon moved to the ladder, tested the bottom rung with one foot, then easily climbed up while I held my breath. He pulled a book gingerly from the top shelf and opened it. To my relief, it didn't fall apart in his hands. He sniffed it. "It's been here for a long time without air-conditioning, but I don't think they're ruined. They just smell kinda funny."

"You smell kinda funny."

"Ha ha." He climbed down. "There's even furniture in here."

I regarded the blocky, sheet-draped shapes in the middle of the room. "Might just be ghosts taking a nap."

"You're a ghost taking a nap."

"Sometimes I feel that way." *Damn it.* I didn't want him to know how invisible I felt most of the time. "I — I'm pretty sure it's not ghosts."

"Coffins?" His tone was light, but his brown eyes held a question. A question for me, not a question about ghosts or vampires.

I pulled a cloth off one of the shapes, and a light-blue brocade settee emerged. At least I thought it was a settee. It was the sort of thing someone like me, whose main experience with furniture was thrift stores and Rooms To Go, would call a settee.

"Must be original to the house." Landon hopped off the bottom rung of the ladder and wandered over to look at it.

The settee was pretty but stiff-looking, and the fabric hadn't held up well. *New upholstery,* I wrote in my notebook. "Definitely not the kind of thing you sit on comfortably while reading a book."

"What's this?" Landon pulled the cloth off another piece. "Library table! Oh, this is excellent work," he said as he examined the corners, carved drawers, elegantly turned legs and what looked like brass casters on its feet so it could be wheeled around. He stroked the wood of the six-by-four table. "Oak, I think."

I pulled a cloth off another blocky shape. "Ah, here ya go."

"Now that's a man's chair," Landon said of the brown leather club chair.

"Is not!"

We exchanged a glance, a challenge, and then we ran for it.

Landon reached it first, laughing, and when I tried to put on the brakes so I didn't crash into him, he grabbed me and pulled me into his lap. "I think there's room for both of us."

"No, there isn't!" I squirmed, but I laughed even harder as he held on tight. Whoa. He had hard, muscled thighs, but that wasn't the only hard thing I felt under my legs. "You win!" I said lamely as I wrenched myself away and tumbled onto an old Oriental rug.

He sat there, still chuckling and maybe just a teeny bit mortified.

"That's a good whiskey-drinking chair," I said as a distraction, then clambered up, dusting off my jeans. When I looked up, Landon was staring at my butt.

Yeah, so much for the distraction. I looked around. "Does that wall look broken to you?"

"Broken?" Landon hoisted himself out of the comfy chair, and I tried and failed not to notice the bulge in his jeans.

Gulp.

He approached the wall in question. On either side of the

stone fireplace were elegant wood panels, a break from the bookcases. "Looks like some well-made wainscoting to me."

"That one looks ... off."

He went closer and touched the indented panels to the left of the fireplace, then pressed his palms against the wood and rattled it.

"Don't break it!"

"I won't," Landon said. "But it doesn't feel right."

"That's what I thought. I mean, it didn't look right. Maybe the house settling pushed it out of whack."

And then he began pushing the wood. Sideways.

"What in the hell?" I came up next to him to stare as the whole panel pushed in and rolled to the left behind a set of bookcases. "It's another door!"

"You mean two other doors."

And so it was. Behind the sliding panel — the pocket door — was a more traditional door, oak with brass fixtures, set back just enough to allow for a doorknob.

"OK, that's creepy," I said. "Closet?"

"Good guess. But why hide it, and behind a second door, no less?"

"Maybe because the sliding door wasn't secret enough. Maybe they wanted to lock it."

He looked at the fluted glass knob, and then he looked at me. "Want to try it?"

I swallowed, reached out my hand gingerly and turned the knob. The door didn't give at all. I pulled out the house key and inserted it into the keyhole. This time, there was no joy, even when Mr. Muscle tried it.

I frowned. I was tired and had to pee. But after seeing this awesome library, I was desperate to know what was behind the door. "Now what? Do we break it down?"

"That would be a shame. It's a beautiful old door, and that

hardware is gorgeous."

"You and your hardware."

"I've never heard any complaints before." He shot me a sideways glance, eyebrow raised.

I couldn't suppress a giggle. "Well, what do we do?"

He gave the door a good once-over. "The hinges look to be on the inside, so we can't pop them ... "

"Locksmith?"

"You're not in a hurry, right?" he asked, and I shook my head. "Then let's try a skeleton key."

"You have a skeleton key?"

"No, but most of these old houses have locks that can be opened with one of just a few keys. That's how they did it back then. You can order them online."

"Seriously?"

"Yeah. I'll order them."

I shook my head. "This is my project. I'll order them."

"My treat. Look, you never know when I'll need them for a house refurb."

"Yeah, while you're building your Tuscan-tropical McMansions."

Landon put a hand to his heart. "That hurt." And actually, he did look sort of hurt.

"I — oh. I'm sorry." I blinked away his hypnotic gaze. "OK. You can order the keys if you want. Now I'm dying to know what's in there."

"You'll find out soon enough. The next question is, what are you going to do with this place?"

"The whole house, you mean?" I took a few steps into the room, sighed and shrugged. "Oh, hell. I have no idea. I mean, look at it. It's a mess."

He glanced around. "It's a treasure."

"The kitchen and bathrooms alone are going to cost a

fortune."

"You can go retro. Get some deals."

"And then what? Live here? I mean, no offense, but I can barely afford to live with you, and I only did that because I couldn't afford my own place and my mom's house is way too small."

"You *own* this place. Plus, you didn't want to live with your mom," Landon said.

"True." My smile was thin. "Not after being a grown-up in the real world." And after my introduction to the real world completely sucked.

"And you like me."

I laughed, pushing down the memory of my disaster in Orlando. After today, I liked him a lot better than I used to. "This is highly impractical."

"Not if you turned it into something. Bohemia would probably welcome this becoming a tourist attraction or a bed and breakfast."

I shook my head. "Bed and breakfast? Cook and do laundry all day long? Not for me."

"You could hire someone to do that stuff, maybe. Or how about an event venue? You do wedding videos, right?"

"Yeah, but — " I didn't want to do wedding videos for a living. But to make a little cash while I made films or had a great video marketing job ... "I don't know if I want to run an event venue."

"You hire someone for the details. It's a business. You borrow a little, make it work. This place is right on the edge of the riverside residential area and close to downtown. I'm sure the zoning board would approve the plan."

"But this ... this place ... I can't possibly borrow enough to fix up this place. I mean, what would this cost to fix up?"

His eyes narrowed, and I could almost see the numbers

flashing in his mental calculator. He shrugged. "Not sure. Half a mill?"

"Half a ... of a *million dollars?*" I sat on the settee, and a spring *sproinged* as I tried to breathe.

He chuckled and set a hand on my shoulder. "I didn't say a *whole* million dollars, but then again, you can spend as much as you want fixing up this place. Maybe a quarter mill if you do it smart. You can do it. The city has some historical preservation grant money it's trying to spend. You can get a business loan. And you can do a really great fundraiser here to get you started. People all over Bohemia want to save this house. If you build it, they will come."

"Like a bake sale is going to save this place." I looked up at him but didn't jiggle too much, because I liked his hand on my shoulder, especially because it had slid toward my neck and was now kneading the knotted muscles there.

"A really good fundraiser gets you seed money. Then you can figure it out. Worst case, you make just enough to get it into salable shape. Though I'd hate to see you get rid of it. It's — it's special." He had a wistful look in his eye.

"Says the home builder-renovator. Though I have to admit that it's charmed me just a little."

Just then, a strange creak seemed to shudder through the room.

"I think the ghost likes you." Landon's eyes twinkled.

"And then there's that." I looked around warily, telling myself that sound was just an old-house noise. "Say I wanted to keep it. I can't build — rebuild this from scratch without a dime to my name. Just for starters, how am I going to get it in shape for any kind of fundraiser?"

He gave my neck a last gentle squeeze, crossed his arms and smiled knowingly. "Me."

CHAPTER 7

*A*fter jury-rigging the mansion's old gate back into place, Landon talked me into lunch at the Diamond. Officially the Double Diamond Diner, it was a mid-century gem in downtown Bohemia with an awesome neon sign and a menu full of hearty classics. I readily agreed, because I wanted to pick his brain. I wasn't altogether assured by Landon touting himself as the secret to my success with Milkweed Mansion.

The business lunch crowd thronged the place, but a friendly waiter found us a two-top. If my friend Millie still worked here, we would've had a nice, cushy booth, but I'd learned the hard way that you have to make the best of what you get.

We both ordered iced teas. I asked for a Reuben; Landon, a burger; and when the drinks arrived, I started my interrogation.

"What makes you think renovating Milkweed Mansion makes any sense for someone as broke as I am?" I asked him.

"It's not a burden," Landon said. "It's an opportunity."

"Taking on something like that scares the hell out of me," I admitted.

"That's because you didn't grow up with my dad. Business is all about risk. If you want to grow, you have to take risks."

"A noble idea, but I took a chance on my first job, and it blew up in my face." I didn't mention that the man who went along with the job assisted in my personal implosion. "I'd rather go with someone I can" — *whoops!* — *"something* I can handle this time around."

He raised an eyebrow as he took a sip of his tea. "Wait a minute. What happened with your first job? You worked in TV, right?"

"Yeah, while I was finishing my master's. I was an assistant director on a new kids' show produced in Orlando."

"That sounds pretty damn good for a first job."

"Doesn't it?" I said wryly. "Only the show sucked, and even when I stepped in as director when the first one left, the boss kept blowing off the ideas I had to make it better. Plus he was an asshole on multiple levels."

Landon's eyes were a little too penetrating. "You had a thing with him?"

"WHAT?" My tone was all protest, but I looked everywhere except at Landon and drained half my tea to avoid a more reasonable answer.

"Sorry. Not my place to ask. But you can tell me."

"We *live* together," I said, "and I don't tell you anything. Why would I start now?"

He shrugged. "You haven't gotten to know me before now."

Ouch. It was true. He was just this hunky guy who came and went, left his socks on the living room floor, and took my checks for half of the rent. He wasn't around much. I'd assumed he was partying all the time, mostly because of his jokes to that effect.

"I haven't given you much of a chance, and I'm sorry about that," I said. "I'm just trying to start over, you know? And no offense, but getting buddy-buddy with the Don Juan of Bohemia isn't really good for my head space."

He chortled. "Don Juan? What do you think I do every

night? I hang out with my friends sometimes, but most of the time, I'm working."

My face heated. "That's not the impression you gave me."

"I enjoy Bohemia's bars, but mostly I'm working."

"What about all the dates you brag about?"

"What about them? The women do find it hard to resist me."

"Gah!" I exclaimed in disgust as he grinned. "And you wonder why I think what I do?"

"You're just so easy." He waved a hand when he saw the steam coming out of my ears. "Not *that* kind of easy. I mean you're so easy to tease. Sensitive, I guess."

My reply was brittle. "Ever think there's a reason I'm sensitive?"

"The guy, right? Your boss?"

"Will you stop *doing* that?"

"What?"

"Reading my fucking mind. Oh, shit." I cradled my face in my hands.

He lowered his voice. "I'm sorry if I upset you, but you can talk to me, you know. I'm not judging you. Tell me about him."

"I don't want to tell you about him. I haven't even told my mother about him."

"She's nice," Landon said. "Maybe you should talk to her."

"I don't want her to know I fucked up the way she did."

Now both of his eyebrows shot up. "You did? Do you — did you have a — "

"No, no." I couldn't help a bitter laugh. "No babies. I know how to use birth control. Of course, the best birth control is saying no to assholes like him. And in case you're wondering, he wasn't married. He was just a guy with a lot of power."

"Power is attractive to girls, I guess." There was something grudging in his tone.

"Hell, no, that's not why I — look. He sold me a line, OK? I hadn't really had boyfriends before him. I was too busy going to school. Getting a master's that so far has turned out to be less than helpful and going into debt besides. If anything, the power difference — him being my boss — was a complete turn-off, and eventually it totally burned me when he blacklisted me with all his contacts in Hollywood. But before that happened, he told me everything I wanted to hear." I bit my lip, trying to shut myself up.

Landon seemed awfully interested in my lip.

I plucked the lemon slice off my iced tea and threw it at him.

"What?" he exclaimed, looking up to my eyes again. "What did he tell you that you wanted to hear?"

"Looking for pointers?" I asked dryly.

"Baby, I don't need pointers."

I couldn't help but laugh, and just then our food arrived, so we spent a few minutes sampling the delicious fare. The sandwich was good, but the fries were perfect, and I knew from past experience they were excellent hangover food.

"So what did he tell you?" Landon pressed after we'd made a dent in the food.

"You want the full guide to seducing Kayla Fetherole?" I couldn't keep the sarcasm out of my voice.

"How about a milkshake?" he asked.

How did he know about my thing for vanilla shakes? "Get out of my head."

"No, really. Can we get milkshakes? My treat. I love them here." The corner of his mouth turned up. "But it's good to know they turn you on."

"Oh, geez." I tried not to be hypnotized by the Fireworks. *Gawd, that smile.* "Shut up. Yes on the milkshake."

"Good. Vanilla OK?"

"Vanilla is mandatory."

Landon chuckled, waved our waiter over and ordered them. "Now tell me what the guy said to you."

"Really?" I rolled my eyes. "I don't want to go into the grisly details, but he told me how talented I was. How he had projects going in Hollywood that I'd be perfect for after we had a couple of years of the kiddie show in the can. He had money and means. He could've made it happen. I killed myself going to school and working for that show at the same time, thinking it was all building to the next step. But right after I got my degree last December, his crappy show got canceled and I got canceled, too. He went back to California, burning down my hopes as he went, telling everyone I was the reason the show tanked."

"But you had a relationship."

"Not like I thought. I think he resented that I had better instincts than he did. He rejected my ideas that would've saved the show. He had an ego as fragile as a moth's wing. As ratings went downhill, I was a constant reminder of his failure. And it turns out the relationship was just him wanting to fuck the latest young fool in his orbit, so there's that."

Landon looked angry and uncomfortable at the same time. "I'm not sure what to say to that. He was a dick. I guess he couldn't resist taking advantage of someone as pretty as you."

"That's hardly flattering." I glowered at him. "He used me. And then all he cared about was saving his reputation at the expense of mine. He was calculating and selfish. Not unlike the Sperm Donor, I figure. The absentee father who had one last way to make sure I didn't get a share of his fortune, and that was to make sure he gave me the worst piece of it."

"Milkweed Mansion?" Landon gave me a sympathetic smile. "It's the jewel in the crown. Worth taking a risk on."

"Optimist."

"Guilty," he said, polishing off his last fry. He looked at me curiously. "Would you want his fortune?"

"No. Not from someone who never wanted me. Though any of old Max Kantera's money would have gone a long way toward helping me get back on my feet. My salary on the TV show was pretty good, but I spent most of it trying to pay down my student loans."

"I'm grateful I don't have those. I took a few courses in architecture and design, but I never got my degree."

"Architecture? Design?" I cocked my head at him. "Why aren't you doing that now?"

"I'd really like to run my own firm specializing in restoring old houses, but I have family obligations."

"Aren't your ideas worth taking a risk on?" I echoed his words.

"Touché. I'll be doing more of my own thing in the future if I get my way. Ah, here we go!" The snowy vanilla shakes had arrived in tall, curvy glasses, the sides gleaming with condensation, the tops fluffy with whipped cream and kissed by a bright red cherry.

I ate the cherry and used the long spoon to scrape off the whipped cream, relocating it to my plate in spoonfuls. I liked whipped cream, but mostly I saw it as a barrier between me and the frozen goodness of the shake.

"What the hell are you doing?" Landon asked. "Give me that!"

"What?" I froze, the last spoonful of whipped cream suspended in midair.

"That!" He nodded at the spoon.

I shook my head and smiled. I stuck out my tongue and leisurely licked all the fluffy cream off the spoon, just to fuck with him. Just to see if I could. His mouth dropped open. Still looking into his eyes, I sucked hard on the straw, and the shake level went down precipitously.

"Shit," Landon muttered, his stare as glazed as a couple of doughnuts.

"Ow. Brain freeze." I closed my eyes and caressed my temples, then looked back up at him. He was ogling my mouth again. "Landon! Yo. What did you mean back there about being my secret weapon in the resurrection of Milkweed Mansion? Why would you even help?"

He blinked and looked up, then took a studious sip of his shake while he regained his composure. "It'll be fun."

"Not a good enough reason."

"Fun is always a good enough reason."

"Hmmm." When had I ever really done anything for fun? It was always about the career. "What's fun about all that work?"

"I like the work. Plus you get to see the transformation. Plus it will be yours."

"Mine." I liked the sound of that. Could this crazy idea actually amount to something? "But you — what do you get out of it? I can pay you something out of the theoretical fundraiser, if it makes any money, but —"

"You don't need to pay me. It'll look great on my resume," he said. "The restoration of Milkweed Mansion? That's a marquee project. In fact, I'm pretty sure I can call in some favors in terms of work and materials if you're open to having a plaque with sponsors' names on it."

"I don't see why not. The plaque might help hold up the walls."

He laughed. "If you're ready to do this thing — "

"The renovation? I — yes. I think so. I don't really have another choice, do I? Whether I want to keep it or sell it. In its current condition, it's a tear-down. Somebody will put a high-rise condo there, and that will be that."

"A depressing thought. My next question is, what's the fundraiser?"

"That's *the* question. What can we do for seed money? Preferably something that won't require massive work starting out. We can't afford to overhaul the whole house right away."

"Plus we might have to hire ghostbusters."

I giggled. Then I sat up straight. "That's it."

"What?"

I was really excited for the first time in a long time. "Halloween is almost here ... "

We locked eyes and said it at the same time. "A haunted house!"

"That's ideal," I added. "So we only need to make the mansion safe, not perfect."

"The worse it looks, the better," Landon agreed.

"But it's still going to be a shit-ton of work. And I need to pay you something," I insisted.

Now it was his turn to *hmmm*. "What if — no strings attached — you agree to go out with me? A token payment."

"What?" First I was shocked, then pissed. I took an angry suck of the shake, and he blanched. "After what I told you about my last experience? I'm not going to be used like that ever again."

"Kayla." He lowered his voice. "I'm not asking you to fuck me. I would never use you. And you'll be the boss — it's your house. Just go out with me. For fun. "

"Do you do everything for fun?" *A date with Landon?* He was planting ideas in my head that made me warm in spite of the milkshake.

"I try. I'll have fun helping you renovate an amazing historic building. You agree to have a fun night out with me. It's all very innocent."

"Ha. Innocent." I eyed him, my thoughts anything but innocent. To tell the truth, his gaze wasn't so innocent either.

"We'll pick the day in advance. Of course, that'll be the day you fall in love with me," he said matter-of-factly, though I detected a twitch at the corner of his mouth.

Laughter bubbled up from my belly and rang in the air so loudly, people turned to look.

"You laugh now." Landon sipped his shake, looking perfectly serious, but humor glimmered just under the surface as he pulled his phone out of his pocket and started tapping. "Let's schedule it for a holiday so we won't forget. Halloween is out, since we'll be busy scaring people."

"You're scaring me."

He ignored me. "Aw, Sweetest Day?"

"You are kidding me, right?"

"Fine. Not that one. Too sappy. National New Friends Day? Ooooh, no, that's a guaranteed Friend Zone holiday."

I laughed again. *"What?"*

"OK, I've got one. October twenty-first. International Day of the Nacho."

"I do like nachos," I mused.

"See? It'll be perfect. And it's even a Friday."

"Wait, if that's the weekend before Halloween weekend, don't we want to have our haunted house open that night?"

"Hmm. You have a point, but I'm worried we won't be done by then."

"We have to be. We can't blow off that weekend." I pulled out my phone and opened my calendar app. "We can do the haunted house Friday to Sunday, then the next week Thursday to Sunday. I figure all the kids will be trick-or-treating Halloween night, which is a Monday, so we probably don't want to be open then, right?"

"If people want to come, they'll just have to come over the weekend," Landon said. "I have an idea. Why not do a VIP party that first Friday night for donors? It'll be another enticement to contribute to the project. Rich people love that kind of thing. You and I can do a date afterward."

"Actually, that's a pretty great idea. How do you know so much about VIPs?"

"I build houses for them."

I squinted at him, a strange thought occurring to me. "If you do such high-end work all the time and you manage projects for the family firm, why do you live in a crappy little apartment, and why did you advertise for a roommate?"

For the first time, Landon looked uncomfortable. "I had to get out of my parents' place. It's huge, and they let me have the apartment above the garage, but I needed my own space. You know?"

"Yeah, but I bet you can afford something a lot better than our cookie-cutter apartment."

"Maybe I could rent something a little better, but I'm saving up."

"For what?"

"To start my own design and renovation firm."

"Ah." I took another sip of my shake. "How does your dad feel about that?"

"He doesn't know yet. But I figure my firm can work with his company if he'll let me. Besides, my two brothers are in the business, too. He doesn't need me."

"I think he needs you a lot, which is why you're anxious."

"I'm not anxious." He sure looked anxious.

I changed the subject. "So about this date … "

"Right! We'll have a date after the VIP party." He glanced at his phone again. "October twenty-first is also National Check Your Meds Day, in case you're interested."

"And *Back to the Future* Day."

"I'd forgotten that!" he exclaimed. "Marty McFly! I love that movie!"

"I've seen it a billion times. *One point twenty-one gigawatts!*"

Landon grinned. "All we need is a lightning storm and we can travel back in time!"

"That's what we have an old house for." A house that I couldn't save without Landon. "OK. Let's do it."

I'm completely insane.

"Excellent!" Landon gave me the Fireworks, and the galaxies did an extra spin in their orbits. "You know, if you want to use *me,* I won't mind," he added. "No woman who goes on a date with me can resist me."

"Ha!" I rolled my eyes again. He might be hotter than a hot plate, but I would resist him. I had to, if I wanted to keep my pride. "You really are terrible."

"Am I?" he intoned suggestively, flashing that smile. *Pow dazzle sparkle.* Damn his Fireworks. They just made me want more.

CHAPTER 8

"Do you want the bad news or the bad news?" Landon said. It was two days after our initial tour of Milkweed Mansion. We were sitting on a couple of folding lawn chairs on the porch, which was the first project he'd tackled while I started cleaning. Now fresh boards created a solid stage here in front and where the porch popped out in the covered hexagon. He'd do the rest of the porch before the haunted house, because we figured there would be a lot of people hanging around outside for the event. That was item number one on a to-do list longer than a Super Bowl halftime show.

"There's bad news?" I asked, knowing the whole house was bad news. It was a hot day, and we were both drinking heavily from our personal water bottles, which Landon kept filling from the giant coolers he kept in his truck. The house still didn't have water or power, so he'd parked a port-a-potty next to the driveaway. It really classed up the joint. On the other hand, it made the bathroom we shared at the apartment seem palatial in comparison.

"Yes, there's bad news." He seemed content as he sat there looking over the grounds in his jeans and dusty T-shirt. In his element. "There's evidence of dry-wood termites. If you don't want the rest of the house to fall down around your ears, we're probably going to have to get it tented."

"Tented?"

"When they cover up the house and pump it full of poison gas."

"Oh, no."

"Oh, yes," he said. "So we're going to lose a few days when that happens, and we'll have to clear the brush that's growing really close to the house before the bug guys even come out."

"How fast can we get someone?"

"Usually you have to schedule weeks in advance, but I'll see what I can do. I know a guy."

I heard my voice get smaller. "And how much is that going to cost?"

Landon took another sip of water from his metal bottle, then looked at me. "I know a guy."

"No, really. No one is going to do that for free. How much?"

He mumbled something into his bottle.

"What?"

"Maybe eighteen thousand dollars."

I dropped my plastic bottle. Since the lid was off, water splashed everywhere. "You're kidding."

He gave me a half smile. "I'm not kidding nearly as much as you think I am. It's about two dollars per square foot. This place is about nine thousand square feet. Ergo ... "

"This isn't happening." I set my bottle upright on the solid new floorboards and stood at the railing, which wiggled under my hands. *Cha-ching.*

"Don't get discouraged." He got up and stood next to me, bumping my shoulder with his.

A volcanic burst of warmth shot through my already hot body, but I shrugged him off, not in the mood for comfort. Or the kind of heat he'd been igniting in my blood since I brought him into this strange house.

I wiggled the railing again. "Why not get discouraged? I can't afford that."

"First, if the termites defeat you, you might as well walk away. This is going to be the first of many battles with the house. For the house. Do you want to do this?"

I looked up at him. Landon was definitely not kidding, and he had an earnest, determined look in his eyes, like he was a knight about to go into battle.

It was disturbingly sexy.

I surveyed the gloomy oaks, the scrubby plants, the ramshackle gazebo and the sparkle of the river in the distance, then turned back to him. "I want to do this."

"Are you *sure?* Because you *can,* but you have to *really* want it."

There was something so confident and reassuring in his gaze, I couldn't help nodding.

"OK, then. I know a guy, and he might want to get on that list of sponsors I was talking about. We'll probably have to pay something, but it won't be terrible."

"It's not *we,* Landon. I mean, I'm really grateful you're going to help me, but I'm the one who needs to pay for this." I mentally calculated what was in my bank account and the limits on my two credit cards. "I'll figure it out."

"We'll figure it out." He smiled then, a lesser version of the Fireworks, this one more reassuring.

"Maybe I'll post an internet fundraising campaign. Just thinking out loud."

"That could help," he said. "You'll need lots of pictures."

"No, I don't think so," I mused. "*Selective* pictures. Let's make it double as a promo for the haunted house. Teasers only. People are curious about this place. No one's really been inside it for more than fifty years. The ghost stories are rampant." I knew this after some intense web surfing. "I'll do a video."

"Now you're talking. But we need to apply for the permit for the haunted house before we start advertising it."

"Oh, great."

"Yeah. Bureaucracy. The construction manager's best friend." He nodded back toward the house. "They'll want to inspect it to make sure it's safe, but I think they'll issue a permit contingent upon us getting the important stuff done. The city has a vested interest in getting this place fixed up. It's been an eyesore for years, plus it's historic. I asked around, and Max Kantera was approached several times about donating the property to the city or simply fixing it up himself."

"And he refused?"

"Saving it for you, maybe?"

"Ha. Not as a gift, that's for sure."

"Maybe as an opportunity. You never know."

A noise from the driveway made us look up. The gate, which Landon had made minimally functional, was open, and a black SUV rumbled down the short lane toward the house. A couple climbed out — a fair-haired handsome guy in khakis and a casual button-up shirt, and a woman with long, chestnut hair in a cute, short floral dress.

"Alex! Sloane!" I called out before trotting down the stairs to greet them with hugs. I'd felt proprietary about this Bohemia Beach couple since I filmed their wedding.

"Kayla!" Sloane pulled me aside as Landon greeted Alex like an old friend. I was starting to think Landon knew everybody. "So this is the man-hunk who's helping you with the house?"

"Shhh. He's not a man-hunk. He's my roommate."

"And a man-hunk," she said, looking Landon up and down. "How's it going?"

"Fabulous. Can't you tell?" I made a sweeping *Wheel of Fortune* gesture.

She laughed, her blue-green eyes sparkling. "This place is charming. Shabby chic."

"Oh, this is way beyond shabby chic. More like 'collapsing in on itself like the house in *Poltergeist*' chic. What are you guys doing here?"

"Alex suggested it. He's always loved this house."

"Does he want to buy it?" I blurted. Alex was loaded. If anyone was going to buy it, he could.

Sloane chuckled again. "No. But I think he'd donate to the cause, if you need it."

"Yes, I would be happy to donate to the cause," Alex said as he and Landon entered our conversation.

"No — that's not really what — I'll take care of it."

Alex nodded. "However I can help, I'd like to. You might need an investor. Don't say no just yet. And I understand you're thinking about doing a haunted house fundraiser here?"

"Yeah, we'd like to." I shot Sloane a look. She'd obviously been sharing our girls' message group gossip with her hubby.

"I'm pretty sure I can help," Alex said. "The permit will be easier to get if it's connected to a nonprofit. I did an informal poll of the board, and the art museum's foundation would be willing to attach itself to the permit. Then you can get a liquor permit, too, and have a bar for the launch party. Those kinds of fundraisers can make a lot of money."

"But — I mean, I love the art museum," I sputtered, "but — no offense — we really need *all* the proceeds to fix up this place."

"We get that," Sloane said. "But you mentioned in your post yesterday that you're thinking of turning this into an event space, right?"

I nodded. "Right. Probably. That seems like the best use, maybe with an apartment for the caretaker."

"Which would be you?" Sloane asked.

"Maybe." I had to admit, since seeing the tower room, I'd had a fantasy or two about actually living here. "I can't afford to make it a museum. But if it's used for events, then everyone can have the chance to experience it once it's fixed up." *If it's ever fixed up.* "What would the art museum get out of helping?"

"The art museum is always looking for unique places to have its fundraisers," Alex said. "In exchange for attaching ourselves to the project and the permit, we'd like to barter for use of the facility for one of those fundraisers down the road."

I laughed. "I love the idea, but you may not be so enthusiastic after you see the place."

He smiled, his gray eyes friendly and keen at the same time. "We'll let you fix it up first."

This time Landon laughed. "You'll have to, unless you want to fall through the floor. But you're going to love the ballroom."

Alex and Sloane were full of questions, so we gave them the abbreviated tour of the first floor so we didn't have to hazard the stairs. While Alex and Landon lingered in the ballroom, I showed Sloane to the library.

The door creaked as we went in, and the whole house seemed to sigh. A high, faraway sound reminiscent of laughter followed.

Sloane's gaze snapped to mine. "What was that?"

I fought back a chill and shrugged. "You tell me."

"Freaky." She took a ginger step into the bookcase-lined room, now brighter since I hadn't replaced the curtains. And then she sneezed.

"Sorry. Old books. When we get the air-conditioning going, it'll be better." *Cha-ching.*

"This is incredible," she said, truly in awe. "It will make a great scene in the haunted house, that is, if you want to open it to the public."

"We can do that. I'm thinking we'd lead tours through and scare the crap out of people at each stop."

"If the house does what it just did every time you open a door, that won't be a problem," Sloane joked.

"Wait till you see this," I said, stopping in front of the sliding panel. I pressed it and pushed it to the side. Landon had oiled the wheels, so it moved with barely a whisper.

"Whoa!" Sloane stepped forward. "What is it?"

I gestured to the door-within-a-door that wouldn't open. "It's locked. We don't know."

"Locked?" she asked in fascination. "How are you going to get in there? Because you *have* to get in there."

"Maybe we can let the skeletons out of the closet for the haunted house."

"Spooky." She tried the doorknob. "Sorry. Couldn't resist."

"Landon's getting some skeleton keys. Apparently a lot of locks in these old houses can be opened by the same types of keys."

"Landon, huh? He's a cutie."

"He's a pain in the ass." With a great ass. I sighed. "Yeah, he's a cutie."

"I could think of worse guys to get sweaty with."

"I'm not getting sweaty with anyone anytime soon," I said, just as I heard a throat clear behind me.

Landon and Alex were standing in the doorway of the library, both of them grinning.

"I beg to differ," Landon said. "You've been getting sweaty with me all afternoon."

Damn it. Sloane came to my rescue as my face got even hotter.

"You know," she said, "if you put out the call, you could get some really creative help on the haunting of your haunted house."

I reset my brain back to the topic at hand and realized what Sloane, a potter who worked at the Bohemia School of Art and Design, was suggesting. Some of the pressure in my head eased a little. "Do you think they would help?"

She smiled. "What artist could resist decorating a haunted house?"

CHAPTER 9

I got in to work Monday morning and immediately went to the corner office and knocked.

"Come in!"

I opened the door to a big space filled with light from the third-floor windows that overlooked the river. Really, this place wasn't so bad. The people were cool. The view was ace. Making video dating profiles — it could be worse, right?

"Kayla," Rick said. "You must be psychic or something. I wanted to talk to you. Close the door. Have a seat."

He wanted to talk to me? I wanted to talk to him about taking what little vacation I'd accrued so I could work on the house.

Rick cast his bright blue gaze around the office for a minute as if noticing his decor for the first time — a couple of surfboards hanging on the wall, a signed poster of Ron Raker surfing a big wave, a Derek Gores collage of a beautiful woman. Then he looked back at me, and I saw something in those eyes I didn't like.

"Kayla, you've done awesome work for us here, and we want

you to keep doing that work. But I'm afraid we're going to have to end your employment."

"What?" I blinked a few times, not quite getting what he said.

"What I mean to say is, if you're willing to work for us on a freelance basis, that's how we'd like to do it from here on out. We're sorting through the in-studio demos. In a month or so, we'll want to start the field shoots to show investors, and we'll call you then."

"You'll what?"

Rick stood, holding out a hand, and I stood in response, a hundred percent stunned, operating totally on automatic, lifting my hand so he could grasp it and shake it with overzealous energy.

"That's my girl. We'll call you soon. Go ahead and take your stuff, though, OK? We need the desk." He walked around me and opened his office door, shouting over the room full of my co-workers. *Former* co-workers. "Maria! Help Kayla, would you?"

Then he gently pushed me out, smiling all the while as he closed the door behind me.

What the actual fuck?

"Kayla? You OK?" Maria had come over to me. The rest of the coders and content creators had gone back to their earphones and keyboards. "You look kind of pale."

"He fired me. I think."

Maria looked around, then guided me back to my desk. "He told me you'd still be doing freelance for us."

I looked around at the oblivious dronebots. They were badly in need of a Nerf war. "Does everyone know?"

"No," she said. "They'll figure it out soon enough. I'm sorry. Are you going to be OK?"

"I guess I'll have to be." And now it was more important than ever that I make the house project work. Or that I get that job with the tourism office, if they hadn't given it away already.

By the time I'd packed my meager belongings in a box and headed to the door, a few of my colleagues were looking up from their monitors wearing curious expressions. Tough. Maybe they'd see me again if I did some freelance for the company, but right now, it was pretty hard to imagine doing Rick's little projects.

Except that I needed the money. I always needed the money.

Well, I got my time off. And I would be spending all of it at Milkweed Manor. Too bad Landon was working his day job right now.

Funny that he was the first person I thought of after my day imploded.

"WHAT ARE YOU DOING HERE?" I asked.

Landon wasn't at his day job. Landon, who now had his own key to the house, was screwing in a new step on the staircase in the grand foyer of Milkweed Manor, his battery-powered drill *zip zzziiippping* in his capable hands as his muscles flexed and those dark eyes squinted behind his safety glasses.

Screwing. Ha ha.

Shut up, id.

I pulled at the neck of my T-shirt — I'd run home and changed into grubby clothes after my humiliation at the office — and blew cooling air into the suddenly warm vicinity of my boobs.

He put down the power tool, pushed up the safety glasses and glanced down the stairs at me. "What did you say?"

"What are you doing here?"

He gave me a brief Fireworks smile as he got up and dusted

off the knees of his well-worn jeans. He came down the steps and grabbed his water bottle, taking a big sip. It was as hot as a volcanic vent in here, even with the front door open. Sweat peppered his army-green T-shirt, which advertised Bohemia Brewing Company and clung nicely in all the right places. Which was all of them.

"What are *you* doing here?" he asked, setting his water bottle down.

"I asked first." I wasn't quite ready to tell him I was out of a job. After all, I had to pay him rent, and I didn't want him to worry.

"My dad loves the idea of me working on the house," he said. "He told me he'd lighten my load for the next few weeks so I can help you get stuff done. He's even sending a crew over later today to help us out. I want to get these stairs stable and make sure there are no holes in the floors before the bug crew comes later this week. They're going to need access."

"The bug crew — a work crew — why? I mean, wow. You got a lot done. But why does your dad want to help?"

Landon shrugged and took another sip of water before putting down the bottle. "I guess he wants to be on that sponsor plaque." He grinned again. "You get the day off?"

"You could say that."

"What?" The grin faded. "What's wrong?"

"Oh, shit. I might as well tell you. I got fired. Well, put on a 'freelance basis,' which is basically the same thing."

"Oh, man. I'm sorry. But you didn't like that job much anyway, did you?"

Landon was more observant than I gave him credit for. "No, not really. But it was a job. And I have to pay for all this. And — and rent, and — "

Damn it. Tears pricked my eyes. I hated crying, but the truth was I cried at almost everything, though I did my best to keep the waterworks bottled up. Usually, I succeeded.

"Hey now," Landon said, coming over and surprising me with a hug. A chill ran through my body. A good chill. My arms apparently acquired minds of their own, because they slipped around his waist without my permission, and he pulled me closer. My body ignored my brain and leaned deep into his snug, comforting embrace as he murmured into my hair, "It's fine. Don't worry about the rent."

"But I do worry." *Oh my God, how can a man this sweaty smell so good?* "I'm just a little overwhelmed right now."

"Shhh." His soft shushing was warm in my hair. "Shhhhhh." Did I imagine it, or did he just *sniff* me?

Holy snotbuckets. We were standing there sniffing each other, rubbing each other's backs, his body hard — *whoa,* even harder against mine ...

I stepped back abruptly before my panties' fire alarm went off and glanced up at Landon's face. He wasn't smiling now. In fact, he looked downright serious. Disturbed. A hundred percent lickable and simultaneously pained, as if he was struggling with something. He managed to paste a dim approximation of the Fireworks back on his face. "It's OK, really. Hell, we'll practically be living here for the next month anyway."

I nodded, not trusting myself to speak.

Living with Landon.

I lived with Landon now, but did I really? He was rarely there, and when he was, at least in the past, he was never really emotionally there. Not that a roommate needed to be emotionally present or anything, but —

OK. I was kind of lying now. Lying to myself. If anyone was absent these last several months, it was me. Because the last thing I wanted to do was get emotionally invested in some hot guy who thought he was God's gift to women.

Or who *I thought* he thought was God's gift to women.

I was really confused right now.

"So you're here to work?" Landon finally said, sounding almost normal.

"Um, yes?"

His smile got real again, and his eyes gleamed. "OK. I've cut some new steps already and routed the edges, but they need sanding. You think you can handle that?"

"Sure," I said. "Just put a tool in my hands and tell me what to do."

"Baby, I've been waiting so long to hear you say that."

I opened my mouth and closed it again, then smacked his arm. And my giggle mingled with his chuckle as he led me over to the workbench he'd set up among the debris that constituted my new mission in life.

"What kind of wood is this?" I asked as he pointed me to piles of cut boards. "It's beautiful. It looks old."

"It's reclaimed wood from an old Florida factory. I thought it was appropriate for the house."

"Where on earth did you get that?"

"I know a guy." Landon smiled. "It's longleaf pine. Sometimes called heart pine."

I blinked at him and tried not to get all squishy again. I was dimly aware of the house sighing around us as I spoke. "That's so — so sweet."

He laughed. "See if you think so after you sand a couple dozen of them."

CHAPTER 10

*T*wo days later, the steps and railings were done. Not *finished* finished, as in stained and sealed, but they were solid, meaning no one was likely to die on the stairs unless the ghost got pissed off.

In addition, Landon's dad's work crew had patched up the floorboards with reclaimed boards where necessary so the bug guys could get in and deploy what I'd been calling the pipes of death.

The bug crew was here working already, even though it was almost sunset. They blasted classic rock from their boom box as they painstakingly used a crane to drape the tall house in huge red- and yellow-striped swaths of heavy fabric and clipped the panels together to make the tent for the termite-killing gas. I'd told them to be careful of the weathervanes, so they were setting up special scaffolding around them to support the tent. The kooky things were a signature of the historic house, and I didn't want them damaged.

"You know, it's a little melodramatic to call what they're doing the pipes of death," Landon said as we walked around the gazebo. Here on the river's edge, the wind gently rustled the oaks and palms, and the water below glowed a pretty gray-blue as the sky turned orange.

We were trying to determine how much work it would require to make the gazebo event-ready. Let's just say that we examined the thing from *outside* the gazebo, because its floor resembled rotten thatch more than it did a wooden platform.

"Pipes of death, I'm telling you. They're piping in deadly poison, aren't they?" I looked inside the gazebo and up. There was a hole in the ceiling, too.

"Well, yes. I think it's more tubes than pipes, though it's not really my area of expertise."

"Semantics. They're going to kill every living thing inside the house. I feel bad for the ghost."

"The ghost isn't living."

"Says you."

A corner of his mouth quirked up. "But at least you didn't have to clear around the house."

"True. And thanks for that." I glanced back at Milkweed Manor, where the weedy foliage hugging the house had been trimmed back to make room for the tent.

"I know a lot of guys," Landon said.

"I've noticed that. When am I going to get the bill?"

"Don't worry about it. They're going on the plaque."

"This is going to have to be a really big plaque."

"Do you mind?" he asked.

"Not if they are donating stuff, no. I'm grateful. But I'm thinking that I can work on the garden myself while the fumigation is happening, since we can't go in the house."

"We have three days. Let's work on the garden far away from the house. Pipes of death give me the willies."

"Ha, see? They *are* pipes of death. Anyway, maybe you should work on this instead of the garden," I said, gesturing to the gazebo. "Can you fix it?"

Landon shook his head. "It might be historic, but I think it's a goner."

"Oh no!" I'd had romantic ideas about the gazebo. "I thought this would be perfect for parties and weddings and stuff."

"Oh, I think you need a gazebo, but the most efficient thing will be to get a brand new one delivered and installed, made of marine-grade lumber and thoroughly anchored against hurricanes. Don't worry. We'll make it retro."

"Cha-ching," I said.

"Already got someone lined up," he said. "I know a guy," he added just as I said, "You know a guy."

He laughed, and I smiled, though mine was on the thin side. "I worry that I owe too much. Owe you. Owe everyone else."

"No one is donating who doesn't want to. In fact, I'm starting to get calls from people I haven't even tried to contact. Word is getting out. Everybody wants to be a part of this project."

"That's pretty cool, but — hey, who's that?"

A hot little red convertible had turned into the lane and was now parking next to all the other vehicles in the drive. A woman with short, dark hair climbed out wearing a business suit as red as the car. She had a big bag, short skirt and heels that were not meant for this Florida jungle. She looked around, decided we were a better bet than the bug guys and made her way toward us.

"You know her?" I asked Landon.

"Jealous?" he teased.

"No! I mean, why? Is she your girlfriend or something?" I looked over at him in alarm, struck by how much I wanted him to say no.

He was choking back a laugh, the rascal. "I don't know her at all. Honest."

The woman, in her mid-thirties, I reckoned, approached with a red-lipstick smile. "Kayla Fetherole?" she queried.

"That's me."

"You own the house, right? I'm from the tourism office for Bohemia and Bohemia Beach. We wondered what we might do to help get the word out about the renovation and the haunted house. People are really excited."

"Uh, really?" I asked. *She's from the tourism office!* All I could think about was the job I applied for there, and she was here about the house. "This is Landon Putter. He's — he's managing the project."

Landon glanced at me in surprise, but he also seemed just a little bit pleased.

"I'm Marla Lyon. Pleased to meet you," she said, reaching out and shaking hands with both of us. "Putter? From Putter Homes?"

"Unofficially, yeah," Landon said.

"Pardon me for asking, but why is the tourism office interested, since the city doesn't own the house?" I asked. "We'd love to get some push for the fundraiser, but —"

"Because this place is a *treasure*," Marla gushed. *All these people calling Milkweed Mansion a treasure have never actually been inside.* "Plus you are doing the city of Bohemia a tremendous favor by turning it from an eyesore into the historic gem it's meant to be. Especially if it's going to be an event space. It could be a tourist attraction as well. We heard you might need a little ... " Marla paused in her enthusiastic monologue, looking embarrassed.

"Money? Help? Therapy? Publicity?" I said. "Yes to all of that."

"We can't provide money, per se, at least not yet. Though I understand you're applying for one of our historic preservation grants" — I looked at Landon in puzzlement, and he gave me a little smile that suggested he'd done me yet one more favor — "and this kind of project is an obvious candidate for those funds.

But in the meantime, we can get the word out to the usual outlets, do some PSAs for you, maybe even — "

"We'd love the help, but you should know I actually have degrees in video production and marketing and plan to shoot some promo," I interrupted her. "In fact, perhaps you saw my resume cross your desk?"

Marla's eyes expanded in surprise. Her brow furrowed. Then the light of recognition dawned.

"Yes!" she said. "Oh my God! *Kayla!* You had a really lovely resume and some very nice footage! But I'm sorry to tell you that another candidate blew us away with his reel. He's had *so* much experience in tourism, we'll be lucky if he says yes."

"So you haven't offered him the job yet? Does that mean I have a shot?" I sounded desperate, but it's not like I looked professional anyway in my grimy T-shirt and shorts.

"Well, no, we haven't offered it to him yet, though he knows he's the leading candidate. Chain of command, you know. Everybody has to sign off on the hire. In fact, it's kind of a funny coincidence, but his dad used to own this place."

I cocked my head at her.

Landon frowned. "Max Kantera *Junior* is your video wunderkind?"

"I thought he was in development?" I asked Landon.

"He used to be, anyway," he said.

"Oh, he's terrific," Marla said. "I mean, if you're curious, I can send you the link to his reel. I don't want you to feel bad. You're very talented, but you'll see he has just the right kind of experience."

My curiosity overtook my ego. "Yeah, that would be great." I slid my business card out of my phone case and handed it to her, since my resume with my contact info was obviously at the bottom of her pile. "My email is on there."

"OK. So. Great!" she said. "Let's set up a meeting and talk about what we can do for the house. When are you available?"

We worked out a time to meet. Free publicity help was better than no help, I figured. And I sort of liked Marla's giddy enthusiasm.

By the time she left, the sun was well and truly down, and the pink twilight was deepening to purple. The bug crew was finishing up its work, and Milkweed Mansion looked like a giant circus tent, ready for tomorrow's fumigation.

And I was in the weird position again of spending all day with Landon and then spending all night with him.

Only not in that way.

Even though I kept thinking about him *in that way.*

"Want to grab a bite?" he asked as we wandered to our vehicles.

The question was casual, but for some reason, a spike of panic shot through me. Because being with Landon was becoming less and less casual. We were sharing intimate space, working together, talking more. He was no longer the annoying roommate I never saw. He was the guy who was helping me turn my life around, and that felt really weird, especially after the last guy I'd entrusted with my future had totally fucked me over.

"I've got to run over to my mom's," I lied.

Or maybe it wasn't a lie, because I suddenly really needed to talk to her.

"OK," Landon said with a smile. Only it wasn't the Fireworks. Did he feel my unease? Did he have his own?

"Thanks, though," I said.

"No biggie. I should check in with the guys anyway. They think I've dropped off the face of the earth." *Dropped off the Bohemia Bar Planet, you mean.* I tried to imagine him doing the rounds, partying, hitting on all the girls, and my tummy flipped.

Did he really do that, or was it all in my imagination? "Kayla? You OK?"

"Huh? Yeah." I nodded emphatically. "Sure. See you later."

"I'll round up some tools tomorrow morning and maybe a few friends, and then I'll meet you here. Time to tend the garden."

There wasn't anything less sexy than pulling weeds on a hot September day. Except, as he drove off and I got in my car, all I could think of was Landon in the garden, naked as Adam on the first day in Eden, beaming his smile at me like the first ray of sunshine.

CHAPTER 11

*I*n the morning, I went to town with the loppers around the edge of the garden, about as far from the pipes of death as I could get, since the exterminators were well into their fumigation by the time I got to Milkweed Mansion. They were wrapping up and leaving me with the giant circus tent around the time Landon showed up.

"Hey," he said casually, setting down a chainsaw, a shovel, a small handsaw and some other stuff. "You look like you've been rasslin' porcupines in the holler."

"Gee, thanks. And this is *not* a holler." I made a couple of warning snips with the lopper.

"I take it back!" He grinned. "What have you gotten done so far?"

"You can't tell, can you?" I looked around. "I actually whacked a ton of these vine things, but there are so many."

"Cape honeysuckle. It's terrific for the hummingbirds and butterflies, but it's a total pain in the ass. Maybe we can just trim it back to the fence. We don't have to eradicate the whole thing."

"I'm pretty sure we can't eradicate the whole thing unless we nuke the site from orbit." I lopped off a few more stems. "I didn't hear you come in last night."

"That's because I didn't."

"Oh." I started clipping more aggressively, and small orange flowers fell around me. *Snip. Snip. Snip.* Where was Landon last night?

"Are you drinking water?" he asked. "It's pretty hot out here already."

"Of course." Though I hadn't been drinking much. I'd been too obsessed with making a dent. Maybe it was the power of suggestion, but the heat seemed to crank up a notch. A wave of dizziness hit me, and I swayed a bit.

"Whoa! Sit down. Here," he said, grabbing my arm and leading me to a concrete bench that had somehow survived the years.

"I'm fine." But I did feel kind of sick. Where did Landon spend the night?

He handed me my Wonder Woman water bottle, and I took a big drink.

"How's your mom?" he asked.

"My mom?" Oh, yeah. I'd told him I was going to visit my mom. And I'd tried. "Turns out she took my grandma to bingo. I just missed them. So I hung out with my Aunt Ginny instead, and she hooked me up with the loppers."

"Always good to have loppers, as long as you use their power for good and not for evil." He shot me the Fireworks.

I laughed weakly and took another drink.

"Matter of fact, I got most of these garden tools from my dad's personal shed," Landon said. "I ended up just staying there last night after dinner. I was so damn tired, I fell asleep on the couch, and by the time I woke up, it was three in the morning. So I just stayed till morning since I didn't want to wake you. I must've just missed you at the apartment."

"Oh, yeah. You must have." I was feeling a little better. "I thought you were going out with the guys last night?"

"School night. They all had work in the morning and didn't feel like it, so I went to my folks' instead."

Funny. I was feeling a whole lot better now. I took another sip, stood and grabbed the loppers. "Hey, have you gotten those skeleton keys yet?"

"Not yet. Slow shipping. We should have them in a few days, about the time it's safe to go back into the house."

"Awesome. I really want to see what's in that library closet."

"So do I. Hey, I asked a tree guy to come out and look at that one leafless oak halfway between the house and the road. It doesn't look very happy. I'm pretty sure he's going to cut it down."

"A dead tree might be atmospheric for the haunted house."

"Not if it *falls* on your haunted house."

"There's that." I frowned. "Isn't it really expensive to cut down big trees?"

"They owe me one. I refer him business all the time. And he wants to be on the plaque."

"We're going to have to melt down the statue in Ponce de Leon Square to have enough brass for this plaque, I think."

Landon laughed. "Hopefully not. Oh, look. The cavalry has arrived."

I looked up, expecting to see a squad of Landon's Known Guys or at least a tree expert, and instead I saw an unlikely crew of a woman and a man in their twenties in shorts and T-shirts, bearing garden tools. "Who's that?"

Landon shot me an expression that suggested I might not like the answer.

"Hey, Landon!" The pretty blonde hugged him first. The guy just shook hands with him, and then they looked at me. "And you must be Kayla," the blonde said warmly.

I began to realize who this was as Landon gestured to the pair. "I ran into Annabel on a job we're doing with her company — "

"Her dad's company," I said without emotion. *My dad's company.*

"The family company." Landon winced. "Anyway, we got to talking about Milkweed Mansion, and she said she wanted to meet you."

"So did I," Andy added. "I hope you don't mind, but — honestly, we had no idea you existed until we read the will. And we want you to know — "

"No hard feelings," Annabel said. "Or rather, I hope you don't have hard feelings, because we really would like to get to know you. I mean, you're our sister."

I was really, really tempted to sit down again, or maybe fake a faint, like one of those women in the historical romances I liked. But my curiosity somehow overpowered my shock and the years of bitterness that had made me hate my father and resent the other life that I knew, deep down, he must have had.

Here was a big part of that other life. My half-siblings. Two of them, anyway.

"I — I'm — I'm not going to say I've never had hard feelings," I admitted. "But I don't have any hard feelings against *you.* How — how do you feel about all this?" I gestured to the circus tent and the oak-studded tropical jungle.

Annabel chuckled. "Bless your heart, Kayla, but I'm glad Dad left you something, and I'm glad you're doing something with it. Honestly, I don't think I'd have the fortitude."

A half smile touched my lips. I liked Annabel's forthright-ness. "Well, that's something. Are you really here to work on this? I thought you had a company to run."

"I told Landon I'd like to help out. This might not be the best way I can help you — I can probably donate some skilled labor when you really get into the renovation — but for now, I thought this might be a nice way to meet."

"And SpaceX owed me a day off," Andy said. "I didn't want to be left out."

"Oh, cool. You work for them?" I asked.

"I'm an engineer. Love it, but it's a ton of hours."

"Rocket launches are one of the coolest things about living here, aren't they?" I was genuinely excited.

Everyone agreed with me, and the ice thawed noticeably between us as we talked about launches we'd seen and how Andy got into the space business. After a few minutes, Landon got them going on clearing a couple of overgrown paths, and I went back to trying to train the honeysuckle into a hedge while Landon used the chainsaw to cut down small nuisance trees.

It was hard to talk during all the noise, so I got into my lopping. By the time Landon's saw stopped, I'd drifted a ways away from my half-siblings, and he wandered over to me.

"So where's my other stepbrother?" I asked him in a low voice. "And why didn't you tell me they were coming?"

"I hope you're not angry, and I'm sorry for springing them on you, but they're actually really cool people, and I wanted you to meet them. I thought it might be better this way. Anyway, it's no surprise they're cool if they're related to you."

"Ha. Flattery will get you everywhere." I stopped lopping, wiped my brow with the back of my arm and squinted at him in the dappled sunlight. "I'm also related to Junior, who Gary said was a tool."

"He is a tool," Landon said, and I laughed. "Not sure if you want to hear this ... "

"What?"

"Max Junior is apparently pissed you got the house. He wanted it, once he found out you got it. Apparently none of them knew their dad even owned this place."

"Why in the hell would Junior want this money-sucking black hole?"

"I think he's the type who wants All The Things."

"Well, he's getting my job, apparently. The one I applied for."

"Has Marla sent you his reel yet?" Landon asked.

"It wasn't in my email this morning." I shrugged. "Not that it matters."

"It matters," Landon said. "What you want matters. I'm mighty curious myself about his heretofore unknown video talents."

"Oh my God," I said, looking over Landon's shoulder. "Is that him?"

We and my half-siblings all looked up at the new arrival, a guy in a slick suit with a product-enhanced haircut who stepped out of a Porsche SUV and surveyed the grounds.

For the record, if I could ever afford a Porsche instead of my ancient Toyota, a hand-me-down from Aunt Ginny, it would be a goddamn sports car. A Porsche SUV? *What's the point of that?*

Anyway, it was clear Max Junior was not dressed for gardening.

He strolled over, exchanged muted greetings with his siblings and Landon, then scanned me with an unmistakable look of judgment on his face.

"So you're Daddy's little love child," he said.

Annabel gasped, and Andy said, "Max!"

I was too mad to be shocked. "I'm pretty sure love didn't have much to do with it. I assume you're Junior?"

"I go by *Max,*" he corrected me.

Which is why I called him Junior.

"If the will hadn't been so clear," he said, "I'd be challenging you in court for this place."

"Stop it, Max," Annabel said. "This is all Kayla got from Dad. We got decades of his love and time."

I swallowed hard, wondering what that must have been like.

"Super," Max said dryly. "Well, I just wanted to see for myself. And I've seen enough."

With one last cold look at me, he spun on his heel and headed back to his Porsche.

Junior was completely absurd. Was his dad — *my* dad — that much of a jerk?

"Later, bro!" I shouted as Max got to his car. He glowered as he slipped behind the wheel.

Landon coughed, covering up a laugh. "I'm sorry, guys, but — "

"I know," Andy said. "I'm sorry, too."

"He misses Dad." Annabel was obviously more forgiving of Max's contempt.

"It's OK," I said. "I can't really get that wrung out over being dissed by your brother. My brother, I guess. I don't know him. But I'm glad I've gotten to know you a little bit. And you've done a hell of a job clearing the path."

"We'll do more, I promise," Annabel said. "This is crazy, but I've always wanted a sister. Please don't be a stranger. I mean it."

Her sincerity got to me a little, or maybe it was the pollen. But I sniffed and let her hug me, and I hugged her back. Andy shook my hand, and the siblings headed for their car while Landon wrapped an arm around my shoulders and squeezed.

"Are you upset?" he murmured as they drove off.

"Weirdly, no." I leaned into him with a sigh. "It's strange to just suddenly have relatives materialize out of thin air."

"Like ghosts come to life?" I heard the smile in his voice.

"Yeah, kind of like that. Do you think Max is going to make trouble for us?"

"If he does, Annabel will kick him in the teeth. But we'll have to keep an eye on him just the same."

I sighed. "I was afraid you'd say that."

CHAPTER 12

The house would be inaccessible for three days. The bug guys left generator-powered fans running to circulate the nasty stuff inside the house, which we heard dimly as we attacked the garden outside the circus tent. With the help of some of Landon's Known Guys — a crew of real landscapers, not my half-siblings — we managed to get the worst of the over-growth under control.

Landon's tree guy came, too, and using a crane and ropes and gymnastics worthy of Ringling Brothers, they took down the dead oak in pieces.

"That was a hell of a tree," the crew's leader, a grizzled guy who looked almost as old as the oak, told us after I'd thanked him profusely. "It probably would've lived another hundred years or so, except I think it got struck by lightning."

"That's a shame," I said. "Look how wide the stump is!"

"Five feet at least," he agreed. "We're out of time today, but if you want us to grind it down, I have an opening next week."

"Not yet," I said. The remaining pillar of wood wasn't just wide; it was at least four feet high. I glanced at Landon. "That might be a great base for some sort of Halloween structure for the haunted house. It could help us do something really big, don't you think?"

He shook his head in amusement. "You're more artistic than I am. Unleash your artist friends on it and see what they come up with."

We didn't plant anything new in the cleaned-up garden, but I asked the mowers to keep one particularly happy patch of milkweed and other wildflowers intact for the butterflies. I liked the idea of using native plants as much as possible. And this was Milkweed Mansion, after all.

That said, once we cleared the vines from the area outside the back door, I found the remnants of a patio and a rose garden. Tough bushes clung to life, and some even still bloomed. One of the landscapers showed me how to prune them properly, and I found myself with a new obsession. I wanted to figure out what kinds I had and which roses I could plant to fill the holes. So in the evenings, I spent what little energy I had left looking up antique rose varieties on my laptop while Landon zoned out watching sports on television. After being together all day, we were weirdly quiet in the evenings, but it was a companionable sort of quiet. I realized that even at night, this was the most I'd ever seen my roommate.

Friday, I checked my girlfriends' online message group, and everyone was buzzing about the haunted house, thanks to Sloane. Ez was in there, too, along with Penelope, a fabulous costume designer; Millie, who ran an event-planning business; Cali, a photographer and Sloane's cousin; and Thea, a graphic artist who made cool sculptures out of paper.

Ez: Can we paint the whole house black?
Me: Not an option. We wouldn't have the time or money anyway.

Ez: But that would look cool.

Me: [*eyeroll emoji*]

Sloane: We need stuff that's cool but also fast and low-budget. Ez, maybe you can be in charge of the music?

Ez: I always get picked for the music.

Penelope: Because you're a musician? LOL. And I'll help with the costumes. Who you going to get to scare people?

Cali: Damien says he's got a whole bunch of volunteers.

Sloane: At least they're all Goth already.

Cali: Not ALL of them.

Penelope: I'm sure I can get some of the theater kids to help.

Millie: Want me to organize the scary rooms? You just have to decide how many.

Me: YES YES YES!

Millie: And you're leading tours, right?

Me: Not me personally. I don't have the right personality. We need actors. Hint, hint.

Penelope: Maybe Jace?

Cali: OMG!

Sloane: OMG!

Ez: You don't have room for that many fangirls.

Penelope: He's not THAT famous.

Me: Have you SEEN the box office for your boyfriend's new spy thriller?

Penelope: He's just regular people, girls. What if he just does the VIP party? He starts rehearsals for his new play in New York the next week.

Me: OMFG. That would be amazing. That will sell tickets like crazy. Not that we're using him or anything.

Penelope: Maybe he likes to be used.

Millie: You are so bad.

Cali: Is it getting hot in here?

Penelope: I'll ask him today. But I'm sure he'll do it.

Millie: Neil asked me about the haunted house ...

Me: Neil from The Junction Box?

Millie: And the Bohemia Bartenders. He says they'd like to do the bar for the VIP party.

Me: Holy shit.

Ez: Now I'm definitely doing the music.

Me: Ghouls. Check. Cocktails. Check. Thea? Anything to add?

Cali: Thea? You there?

Thea: Sorry. I was talking to Duncan. He says he can vlog the opening night VIP party so you get more exposure.

Me: THAT WOULD BE AMAZING!

Thea: And I have some ideas for sets, if you let me see inside.

Me: It'll be safe to go back in the house Sunday. Maybe you can come over?

Cali: I want to come over! I want to shoot it before you make it all nice!

Me: Ha ha ha. You have plenty of time.

Penelope: I want to come over too.

Ez: Ditto ditto ditto we all want to come over.

Me: That'll work. We're taking Sunday off before we kill each other.

Ez: With sex?

Me: WITH WORK. How about a picnic Sunday afternoon on the grounds? Just warning you, the only bathroom is a port-a-potty.

Penelope: Love it! The picnic, not the port-a-potty.

Sloane: We'll survive. I'll bring some apps.

Millie: I'll set up a spreadsheet and we can all sign up for stuff.

Me: You all are the BEST! How can I ever thank you guys?
Sloane: Bring Landon.
[*chorus of gooey hearts and heart-eye emojis*]
Me: Shut up. I'll bring Landon.

EXCEPT FOR MY COUSIN GARY, I'd only really gotten to know these people better since I moved back to Bohemia from Orlando, but were they great friends or what?

Whatever food they didn't cook for the picnic, they shopped well for, and Gary even filched a charcoal grill from his mom's house at my suggestion so we could grill up some chicken and steaks and mahi. We'd scraped together some folding tables and chairs with mismatched tablecloths and set everything up under the oaks and palms near the river.

Landon quickly made friends, as was the Landon way, and soon he was drinking beer and joking around with not just Gary and Alex, but video blogger Duncan (who came with Thea), sand sculptor Bennett (with Millie), and pro surfer Wyatt (with Cali). Landon seemed completely unintimidated, even by the most famous of the bunch, Penelope's actor boyfriend Jace. I wished I had that kind of comfort with people, but this crowd made it easy even for me.

Except for Thea, who was enjoying a Bohemia Brewing Company ale, the rest of the gals were carrying around clear plastic cups with a bold cabernet as we wandered through the recently cleared paths of the garden.

"So what's this? A UFO landing site?" Thea, her curly red hair loose and wild in the warm afternoon breeze, was staring at a big, round, dark spot in the yard near the cliff.

I regarded the obvious gap in the landscape. "That's where the gazebo used to be. Landon got someone to take it away yesterday."

"Aw, that's too bad," said Cali. She had a camera over her shoulder and her straw-colored hair in a ponytail. "Wish I'd gotten a shot of it."

"I'm sorry. It fell apart as soon as the front-loader touched it," I said. "I got a couple of video shots, and it's 4K, so I can pull pictures off of it for the historians. We're having a new one delivered before the haunted house. Donated. Someone Landon knows. He seems to know everyone. And he already has permits in the works for everything. We're supposed to have electricians and plumbers out this week to get the basics taken care of."

"Landon, huh?" said Penelope, whose pretty blond hair had a pink streak and whose pink retro dress had white polka dots. There was a gleam in her green eyes when she mentioned my roomie.

I raised an eyebrow back at her. "He seems to think renovating this place will be a feather in his cap. I have to admit, there's no way I could do this without him. But don't get any ideas."

"You're the one who should be getting ideas," said Ez, pushing her dark hair out of her eyes.

"I think she is. She's getting all red," said Millie, whose Betty Boop cheeks were pink, too.

"Am not." I totally was. I could feel the heat in my face.

"Leave Kayla be," Sloane said. "Time will tell."

I snickered. "Yeah. We might kill each other before this is over and populate the house with real ghosts."

"Kayla!" Sloane said while the others laughed.

"So when do we get the tour?" Penelope asked.

"How about now? Do you all mind if I film a little of it?

Maybe get some moody silhouette shots and the occasional scream?"

Thea let out a blood-curdling scream that made us all jump and had the guys running over. "Just practicing," she said, the corner of her mouth turned up.

"You scared me to death, darlin'," Duncan said in his adorable Scottish accent.

"We thought we'd do a tour," I said. "Landon, do you want to take the lead? I'll bring up the rear so I can get a few shots."

Landon bestowed us with the Fireworks. "I'd love to. Let's leave the library for last, OK?"

"Sounds good." I shot him a questioning glance, wondering what he was up to. I grabbed my video camera out of the car as the others deposited their beverages on the picnic tables and gathered on the porch.

At our request, since the forecast was dry, the bug guys had left the windows open yesterday morning when they'd removed the tent, so there had been plenty of time for the poison gas to dissipate. The house felt eerily quiet as we went through the rooms, much as Landon and I had done when we first toured the house, only this time there were no treacherous holes in the stairs or floor.

Cali snapped photos, exclaiming over the appealing decay of the kitchen and the upper bedrooms, while I shot some moody video at Dutch angles, capturing feet climbing stairs, creaking doors and the occasional scream on demand. At one point in the tower, Thea and Penelope had a scream-off that had the guys running for cover and the rest of us holding our ears, until the whole house seemed to creak and sigh, shutting everyone up.

"I have a second sense about these things," Penelope said, "and that was fucking weird."

"Maybe we shouldn't scream anymore," Thea added.

"That's ridiculous," Ez scoffed. "There's going to be a lot of screaming for the haunted house anyway."

"I just don't want to make fun of them," Penelope whispered.

"Who's them?" Sloane asked, looking alarmed.

"Stop it," I said. "You're freaking me out. Let's get down to the library. I think Landon has something in mind."

When we got down there, the women who hadn't seen the library yet ohhed and ahhed while Duncan handed out cups of whiskey. "From my dad's distillery," he said. "The good stuff."

"I told him it was kind of an occasion," Landon explained to me as we crowded into the room.

"It is?" I asked.

He showed his dimples, reached into his pocket and produced a brass ring. From it dangled a handful of antique-looking keys.

"You got the keys!" I shouted and leapt over to hug him, almost knocking him in the head with my video camera. And then I gingerly (and reluctantly) released him after hearing the chuckles behind me. Embarrassed, I turned to address the others. "I should explain. These are very special keys."

"Uh-huh," Ez said, knocking back her whiskey and holding out her cup for another. Duncan filled it with a grin.

"Are you going to open it?" Sloane sounded more excited than I was.

"I hope so," Alex said, wrapping an arm around her.

"What are you all talking about?" Thea asked, leaning into Duncan.

"The secret closet!" I said.

There was a satisfying burst of excitement in the room. Cali started fidgeting with her camera settings and nudged Wyatt to get his phone ready to shoot, too.

"Maybe you shouldn't," Penelope said. "Out of respect."

"Respect for what?" Jace said, slipping an arm through hers.

"The ghosts," she said, met by nervous titters.

"I respect the ghosts," I said, "but we are going to open this closet."

"Which is where?" asked Gary, who had an arm wrapped around Ez. All the couples were girding themselves for whatever was behind that wall, it appeared.

I wasn't in a couple, but I sure was grateful for Landon at that moment. I nodded at him, and he went to the paneled wall, pushed, and rolled the outer door to the side.

"Whoas" and "wows" filled the room.

"Do you want to open it?" Landon asked me. "I measured the pin in the keyhole, and I'm pretty sure one of these keys will work."

I swallowed, starting to feel a bit nervous myself. I hoisted my video camera instead. "You go ahead. I want to film it."

"Jesus, it's not like it's King Tut's tomb," Ez said as the others laughed.

Landon chuckled, too, chose a key on the ring and inserted it in the keyhole.

He tried to turn it. Nothing happened.

"I think your key has performance anxiety," Penelope joked to laughter.

"Never," Landon answered, and the guys laughed again.

He looked closely at the keys on the ring and inserted another one in the lock. For a second I thought he had it, but it wouldn't turn.

"Now this is getting embarrassing," he said as we all chuckled. "I need another whiskey."

Duncan obliged him with another shot, and Landon gulped it with a satisfied sigh and handed the cup back to him.

"OK," Landon said, picking out another key. "If this doesn't work, we might be in trouble."

"If it does work, we might be in trouble," I murmured, trying to hold my camera steady in spite of my jitters.

Landon slid the key smoothly into the keyhole, gripped it firmly and slowly rotated his wrist.

The *snick* echoed in the sudden silence as we held a collective breath.

I lowered the camera as Landon looked straight at me, his eyes sparkling. "It's unlocked."

CHAPTER 13

"*I*t's unlocked." Landon's quietly jubilant words filled my ears. My stomach quivered. We were about to see what was in the secret closet. Was it treasure? A creepy doll collection? An actual skeleton?

"Well, come on!" Sloane said, and her cry was soon echoed by everyone else in the room.

Landon beckoned me over. I couldn't resist the chance to open the door. I thrust my video camera at Wyatt, who was a photographer as well as a surfer, and he stuffed his phone in his pocket, grinned and started shooting. He and Cali were double-teaming this. It would be the best-documented secret closet opening ever. All of a sudden I felt like I was on one of those dumb ghost-hunter shows.

As I sidled up to Landon, some in the room stepped forward; one or two stepped back. I put my hand on the glass doorknob and looked up at him, frozen in the moment. He gave me an encouraging smile, warmer than the Fireworks, and put his hand over mine, sending a zing of awareness through me.

Together, we turned the knob and pushed.

The dark space beyond exhaled into the room. It was a cool

sigh that was echoed by the house, with a creaking and that distant tinkling that seemed like more of a suggestion of sound than an actual noise. I dimly registered that everyone in the room looked just a tiny bit freaked out as they gasped and cursed.

"Do you have the flashlight?" Landon called, and Gary handed him a compact metal flashlight. "Ready?" Landon asked me.

"Turn the damn thing on."

Landon clicked on the crazy bright LED beam and swept it around the space.

At first I thought the emptiness went on and on, like a tunnel, and a thrill shot through me. But then I realized that Landon wasn't illuminating a passageway. He was basically illuminating ... nothing.

"What's in there?" asked Sloane, who was right behind me.

"Um." I didn't want to admit it was nothing.

"Nothing?" Ez guessed. She was right behind Sloane.

"Maybe?" I said. The sudden adrenaline crash that accompanied my disappointment made me woozy. I touched Landon's arm and took the flashlight from him, sweeping it around. It was a closet, all right, about the size of my small closet in our apartment. The walls were made of roughly put-together boards that were dark with age. Nothing was in the corners except dust and a couple of vacant spiderwebs.

"Wait," Landon said. "Let me have that again."

He took the flashlight back and shone it upward, toward what appeared to be an empty shelf. "There's something here," he said.

The shelf was high, and he was taller than I was. "I can't see it."

"Books," he said. "It looks like a stack of books. Four — no, five of them."

"Books? In a library? That's crazy talk," Thea said.

"Smart-ass," I said under my breath, and Sloane laughed. "Can you get them?"

Landon handed me the flashlight again, and I shone it upward as he stretched up and reached back. The shelf was deep, and it took him a second to drag the books forward and over the edge.

A cloud of dust followed, and Sloane and I stumbled back, coughing. Landon stepped out of the closet with the books in his arms and headed for the library table. The others gathered around — though not too close, as another pyroclastic flow of dust exploded out of the volumes as Landon set down the books with a heavy *thunk*. He dusted himself off, unperturbed by the dirt.

After the last few days in the garden, we were pretty much immune to dirt.

I joined him at the table and stared at the top book on the stack.

It was a little smaller than the others. The cover boards were wrapped with marbled paper, much worn, with brown leather at the corners and on the binding. I reached out and flipped open the cover.

On the first page, printed in a typeface that evoked the nine-teenth century, was the word RECORD surrounded by flourishes.

I turned the page again and was surprised to see lines and lines of words and numbers — lists. At the top of the first page, written in a neat hand, it said *1896*. The next line said *Family Expenses October*. Below that were lists of purchases with impossibly tiny prices next to them — needle and thread and cotton fabric. Onions and lemons. Wages for the servants and payments to the milkman.

"That's pretty neat," said Alex, who'd come to peer over our shoulders as most of the others, sensing the main show was over, chatted and checked out the other books in the room. I noticed Cali taking a few photos of us, but then she also stepped back, and Wyatt had stopped filming.

I had to admit a ledger wasn't all that exciting. Maybe the ghost was an accountant.

"Probably kept by the lady of the house," Landon said, as if reading my mind.

"Their computer must have been broken," I joked. "My God, this is a lot of detail."

"It's what you did back then if you had a big house to manage," Alex said.

"Let's see what's in the other books," Landon said.

I closed the ledger and set it aside, then opened the next book. It was bigger, but it was more of the same, as were the third and fourth books. Though about halfway through the third book, the handwriting changed, and the entries didn't seem quite as methodical.

I traced the less elegant letters, wondering who had written them. "What a weird thing to save through the centuries. You'd think one of the residents since then would have thrown it out."

"I have a feeling no one even knew about that closet after the original residents," Landon said. "It was hidden behind that panel. It's totally a fluke that we found it."

"But why would anyone even lock these up? It's so strange."

"See what's in the last one," Landon said.

"No doubt riveting accounts of the cost of nails," I replied.

"Nails are *fascinating*," Landon said, and Alex chuckled before wandering over to join the rest of the group. I could hear them batting around words like *skeletons* and *coffins* and *blood*. This was really happening!

I turned my attention back to the fifth book. It was not exactly the same as the others. Its cover was entirely made of gently worn red leather and tooled with a floral design. JOURNAL was typeset on the first page, and it was written in the same elegant hand that was in the first ledger, but it didn't list household supplies.

October 7. Sunny and warm. A little rain. We planted the first roses. With good fortune and weather, our garden will be as lovely as the one we had in New York.

"The rose garden," I whispered.

"Looks like a gardening journal," Landon said with interest, turning a few pages. "This Wickham she mentions — he must be the gardener. And there's a Stanford and accounts of his tribulations with pineapples."

"That's right! I read that the Fountain family owned a pineapple plantation on the beach."

"Good luck finding pineapples over there now."

"That's a little sad, isn't it? I want to take this book home. Maybe it'll tell me exactly what the roses are out there."

"Good idea," Landon said. "Should we leave the rest here?"

"Might as well. The historical society might be interested. If we show them we care about the history, maybe they'll stop calling me every three days to make sure I'm not going to knock down the house."

Landon chuckled. "That Motebarkle guy, right?"

"He means well."

Full of soft light, Landon's gaze held mine as the golden hour took shape outside the big windows. "Are you disappointed?"

I got lost in those deep brown eyes for a moment.

"Not at all," I said, not at all sure I was talking about the closet and the books. "Thank you."

"No problem." He slipped the correct key off the ring and slid it into my hand. The feel of his rough skin against mine shot goosebumps up my arm. "You'd better hang on to this."

CHAPTER 14

I put the skeleton key on my keychain more for good luck than anything. And maybe because touching it made me think of things — of someone — I really shouldn't be thinking of.

It wasn't like I'd need the key anytime soon, though we relocked the closet to keep snoopers out. We had way too many renovations to think about for me to waste time researching the strange closet.

While Landon worked miracles with the city's building department and his crews of Known Guys to get the renovation and event permits we would need, I spent an afternoon editing together a promo video from our friends' visit to the house. It was a teaser more than anything, with judicious cuts that implied more than it showed. I combined slow-motion glimpses of blurry figures, dilapidated rooms, spooky staircases and creepy shadows with light effects, a dash of scary music and one of Thea's amazing screams. It concluded with effects-laden titles: *MILKWEED MANSION unlocked ... experience Bohemia's original haunted house!* I included the dates and a web address at the end for a quickie site Thea and Cali had agreed to put together. October was less than a week away, and we wanted to announce everything on the first of the month.

And I was freaking out just a tiny bit. Landon and his peeps were a massive help, but my bank account was dwindling anyway. I had to put enough aside for the basics of living, and I'd received my last paycheck. Plus I kept having to dole out money for supplies, or pizza for the helpers, or any number of little emergencies.

Tuesday evening, Landon was watching some sort of football analysis show from the couch — hey, it beat politics — while I sat in the easy chair and stared at my credit-card balances and bank account on my laptop. As I willed one set of numbers to go down and the other to go up, I realized he was calling my name.

"Kayla? Is something wrong?"

I looked at him bleary-eyed and saw my fatigue reflected in his handsome face. It wasn't just work on the mansion wearing him out. I knew he'd also been popping in to help on jobs with his dad's company, even though his father had pretty much given him *carte blanche* to help with the house. I didn't understand why, but I was grateful.

"I just don't think I can handle this alone," I admitted to him. I could have put on a brave face, but I was just too damn tired.

"You're not," he said with a small smile.

"No, I'm not, thanks to you and everyone else. But there are still expenses. We can't get everything donated. Permitting fees … the electrician's supplies … paint for the whole house … "

"That'll come later, and anyway, I think I know … "

"You know a guy?"

"A girl, actually. I mean a woman. She owns a paint company on U.S. 1. I think she'd love to be on the plaque."

I was so tired, I didn't even worry about whether this paint lady was just a friend or a passionate paramour. And I'd been thinking a lot along those lines lately, when the last thing I wanted was to be jealous about Landon.

"It just feels weird to take all this money," I said, "and I *am* paying you rent. There are no two ways about that."

"It's OK, Kayla. You can pay me rent if you want to." He flashed me the Fireworks.

I couldn't help a pathetic little laugh. "Easy for you to say."

He looked thoughtful. "Why not reconsider Alex's offer to invest? He's jazzed about the event space, and he loves supporting local art and history. This is right up his alley."

"I don't know. It feels like taking charity. And what if he wants control?" Because even though I'd been reluctant to take the project on, the idea of running the business had grown on me. As Landon had suggested, it was *mine.*

"That's what contracts are for," Landon said. "And believe me, it won't be charity. He has a nose for profit. Not that you don't have any business sense — "

"It's not my strong suit. Yet."

"I'm just saying he has a gift for picking projects that work and turning around projects that don't. And I didn't want to bring it up, but if you need more money, my dad was feeling me out about investing, too."

"Really? What would he get out of it?"

"I honestly don't know," Landon said. "The plaque?"

I chuckled. "I'm sure that's it." I wasn't convinced yet that an investor was a solution, but my burden felt a little lighter just talking to Landon. "OK. I'll think about it."

"Good. Now put down the computer and come over here."

I wrinkled my brow at him. "Why?"

"Why so suspicious? Because you need to relax, that's why."

Every molecule in my body pulled me toward the couch. It was like I was a meteor and the couch was the black hole. Only it had this glowing light at the center. Fireworks.

I closed my laptop, set it on the coffee table and sank with a sigh into the cushions next to Landon.

"Here," he said. "Turn your back to me."

"What?"

"Trust me. I don't bite."

What if I want you to? was on the tip of my tongue. Which I bit to keep it quiet. I turned sidesaddle on the couch, and he touched my shoulders lightly, caressing them through my T-shirt. I knew this was innocent, a little massage between friends, but every cell he touched lit up like pegs in a Lite Brite. His touch became more deliberate, more delicious, until he was digging into the rigid muscles like a pro, rubbing away my worries with his fingers in slow, circular, magical motions.

I hadn't realized just how much I ached until the tension started to melt away under his skilled touch, until he dug deeper and massaged the base of my neck and the center of my back. My head drooped, and I groaned.

Oh, shit.

In response to my guttural sound of pleasure, Landon made a noise at the back of his throat and shifted slightly behind me. What must he think? That I was totally turned on and just waiting for him to jump my bones?

Because let's face it. That's exactly what I was thinking.

He smelled like his soap, that cedar-citrus aroma, like a forest studded with lime trees. Enhanced by the warmth of his body, which suddenly seemed closer and warmer than ever, the scent was completely intoxicating. Before I even realized what I was doing, my body was drifting back against him — whether in a sleepy dream or completely awake arousal, I couldn't testify — and his hands slipped down from my shoulders to curl around my waist.

He didn't say anything. But his warm breath against my neck set every nerve on fire. My nerves were like those little plastic players in that old electric football game, buzzing and vibrating and going every which way.

"Landon?" I whispered.

His arms drew me closer against him, against every hard angle of his body, including one particular angle as hard as a two-by-four (and possibly as large, given its prominence). His warm lips brushed against the skin under my right ear, and my senses exploded.

An unsteady musical breath skirled out of me and up to the stars as I leaned my head sideways to give him access. He took my invitation, laying open-mouthed kisses against my skin there, licking the delicate shell of my ear, tugging at it with his teeth. Molten heat shot right to my honeybun.

What am I doing? I was scared shitless. I was in too deep. I was loving it.

He deftly turned me, lifted me so I was in his lap. His eyes were hooded, and I closed mine as I leaned in close, in denial that this was happening, wanting so much more. He grasped my face with both hands and crushed his lips to mine.

Holy leaping narwhals! My mouth blazed like a sparkler on a birthday cake, all hot flecks of light and butter and sugar. I opened to his tongue, moaning again, and this time he growled in answer as he slid one hand up my waist, under the soft cotton of the tee. He traced the lower curve of my breast with one finger so slowly I thought I'd scream. I had de-bra'd as soon as I'd had my shower, of course, because we were *platonic roommates, for God's sake!* And now my nipples tingled, turning diamond hard as his tantalizing, rough fingers inched closer to the aching peaks.

And that's when I came to my senses and pushed him away. Only he didn't move, and my push ended up toppling me off his lap and onto my ass on the floor.

"Ouch."

"Kayla, are you all right?" was Landon's first reaction, though it was more than concern I saw in his face. He was flushed and breathing hard. I resisted looking farther down, except I couldn't help myself, and then I snapped my gaze back up to his, trying not to think of that big beautiful thing he was hiding in his shorts.

"I'm fine," I croaked, scrambling up and stepping back.

"Are — are you sure? Come back here and take it easy."

"No. No, I can't do that. We shouldn't do this."

"It's totally natural, Kayla."

"Duh, I know sex is natural!"

He let out a little laugh. "Yeah, but what I mean is, we've been spending all this time together, and I like — I like working with you. It's natural we should have a little attraction, right?"

A little attraction? I'd been ready to let his rocket ship blast into my spiral galaxy.

"This is a bad idea. We're working together." *And I don't want to be another notch on the virtual Landon bedpost.*

Yes, I do.

No, you don't.

"Oh, shut up. I mean, me, *me! Me* shut up. *I* need to shut up and go to bed," I said. He looked confused and — hurt? Was he hurt?

"We're not working together like employees. We're working together like — like friends," he said.

Yeah. *Friends.* Somehow that word stabbed a dart into my heart. "Landon, you're the best — I mean, that was fantastic, but I have a meeting in the morning. I'll talk to you later."

And I grabbed my laptop, retreated to my bedroom and slammed the door, feeling like a complete idiot.

A completely horny chicken-shit idiot who wanted to fuck Landon until the ghosts rose from their graves.

CHAPTER 15

*M*y cowardly behavior continued the next morning, when I did my routine in the bathroom before Landon woke up, then hid in my bedroom, getting ready for my appointment with Marla the marketer, until he left the apartment. I just wasn't ready to face him after our close encounter the night before. How was I going to work with him every day? And how awkward would our *Back to the Future* Nacho Day date be now?

I checked my email over coffee before I headed out and saw Marla had sent me something. It was the link to Max's reel, the one that had all but nailed the video marketing job for him. It irked me that someone who was such a prick was getting the exact job I wanted, but I couldn't help looking at it before I left the house.

I had to admit, it was slick. Most of the clips were from other counties in Florida. He must've been doing work for a few years to get these kinds of shots — hot-air balloons, horseback riding with cowboys, a rainbow over shells on the beach, shoppers, divers, glass blowers, outdoor dining, the usual kinds of tourism things. There were even some sexy drone shots of tourist spots. Maybe he'd been an intern somewhere? Because I sure didn't know his name before now, and I'd done a lot of networking with my classmates and other video and TV people when I worked in Orlando.

I shot the link to a couple of the people I'd been in grad school with and a teacher I really trusted to see if they'd heard of him. Maybe I needed to work at the same places Junior had. I could use this kind of video under my belt if I wanted to throw myself into video marketing ... especially since Hollywood was off the table thanks to my asshole ex-boss/ex-seducer.

I sighed and finished my coffee. It wasn't the time to beat myself up. It was time to enlist Bohemia's help in marketing the haunted house.

My Toyota grumbled but cranked up as usual, and I made it to downtown in about fifteen minutes. Though we lived in an unremarkable apartment complex away from the historic downtown, I had ambitions to live closer to this thriving hive of art and commerce. In a mansion? Too soon to say, but I loved being near the Bohemia School of Art and Design, galleries like Cali and Wyatt's, great bars and restaurants. Bohemia had grown a lot since I was a kid here, and I really liked the energy of the place.

The tourism office wasn't all that far from Milkweed Mansion. It took up one suite in a seven-story building south of the main causeway bridge that crossed the lagoon to Bohemia Beach.

I met Marla in the conference room. One wall was lined with big photos of the river, the beach, downtown Bohemia in Christmas lights, a nighttime rocket launch. Windows made up the opposite wall, and the view did not disappoint.

"Oh, Marla." We'd been talking for thirty minutes about

strategies for marketing the haunted house, and I kept looking out at the dazzling water. "I sure wish I could've worked here."

"Actually," she said as I turned back to her, "I kind of wish that, too, but I'm not in charge, and you have to understand that Max's reel blew everyone away. Plus my boss was friends with his father ... " She blanched when she realized what she'd said; the gossip mill had wasted no time in revealing how I'd inherited the house from *his* father. *My* father. "Well, anyway, he didn't even have to interview. I like you. I think you'd be great. And this haunted house promo video is terrific."

"Thanks." We'd hooked up my laptop to their network so she could roll my video on the big TV in the conference room. It *was* pretty damn good. "So you'll run our press release up the flagpole?"

"Yes, and we should be able to get it approved and sent to the *Bohemia Bugle,* local radio and the Orlando TV stations on Friday afternoon, since October starts on Saturday. Will that work?"

"Sure," I said, making a mental note to ask Thea and Cali to rush the website by one more day. If they were still talking to me when this was over, it'd be a miracle.

"Great," Marla said. "I'm sure the TV folks will love covering a haunted house that's not in a theme park, especially with this video to show."

"I hope so." I had my doubts, but getting curious Orlando tourists to come to our coast for our fundraiser would be great.

"I also asked the Bohemia Historical Society president to give me a quote on the historical significance of the place to put in the release, and he says he wants to do a piece about the house on his radio show."

"Ken Motebarkle? Well, that's cool," I said, then noticed the funny look on Marla's face. "What is it?"

"He doesn't approve of the haunted house, but he says he'll

give me the quote to help save it. That said, I'm not really sure how nice his radio show is going to be."

"Oh, good lord. One moment he's calling me asking me not to knock it down, and the next he's complaining because I'm not letting it fall down?"

She sighed. "He'd like it to be a museum. I see his point, but this way it'll sort of be living history that everyone can enjoy. Right?"

"Absolutely. Our goal is preservation, not obliteration. It's not like it'll be a haunted house *all* the time." *Except for the strange sounds and weird chills.* "If the permits are approved, I promise I won't turn it into a condo *or* a convenience store."

She laughed. "You didn't hear it from me, but you're going to get some very good news on that front today, contingent on the house passing initial safety inspections. The mayor has lit the fire under everyone involved in this project. With her on the case, you basically have the blessings of the angels."

"Really? That's so — so *nice.*" To my embarrassment, tears welled in my eyes, and I wiped them away. "Damn it. Sorry. I'm just not used to people being so kind and helpful."

She shrugged and smiled. "Just a suggestion, but it wouldn't hurt to send the mayor and my boss tickets to the VIP opening."

"And you! I'll be glad to. With all the help you're giving me, I'm hoping we'll sell out."

"You will," she said warmly as she rose, smoothing her suit. It was time to go. "And stay in touch. The next time a job comes open here, I'll make sure you're at the top of the list."

I left the meeting feeling a little better about our project, though I still didn't know how I would pay for all of it. As I popped out of the elevator into the parking garage beneath the building, my phone started buzzing in my big bag, and I cursed and struggled as I dug past my laptop and all my junk, trying to get it. I didn't even have time to register the caller ID before I gasped, "Hello?"

"Kayla! Glad I caught you." *Rick the CEO.* "Remember I said I wanted to do some of those prototype dating interviews in the real world? Well, I need one ASAP for a surprise visit from one of our investors. Do you think you can get one done by Friday noon? I want to get it staged on the app. You have all the gear, right? I can pay you … "

He quoted a figure that would cover my part of the rent this month and a couple of pizzas besides. As pissed as I was at the oblivious goofball, I couldn't say no.

And he wanted it *when?* "Did you say Friday at noon? I have to shoot it and edit it, but I guess I can get it done. Who did you have in mind as your dater?"

"We don't have enough time to schedule one of our alpha testers. You know people, right? Anyone will do. Only make it interesting, OK? If they're boring, then make shit up. Oh, and they shouldn't break the camera, if you know what I mean. Ugly doesn't sell. Ha ha. We're emailing you the title templates now. Let Maria know when you've sent it to the FTP, all right? Thanks."

And he hung up.

"Bastard!" I exclaimed. I looked around to see a guy emptying trash cans who gave me a sour look. I waved at him meekly and got to my car as quickly as possible, slipped inside and shut the door. "Fucking bastard!" I screamed in the relative privacy of the sedan. The dude wanted me to turn the video around in a day and didn't even have a victim for me? "MALE PRIVILEGED ASSHAT!"

I closed my eyes and took a few deep breaths. Now I felt better.

I needed a plan. I needed to interview an *interesting* single person for this video. And fuck Rick for judging people for their looks, but he wanted someone attractive, too? Where was I supposed to find this unicorn at such short notice? I had friends here now, but not one of the annoyingly lovey-dovey dopes was single.

Except maybe one.

CHAPTER 16

"*Y*ou want me to do what?" Landon asked later that afternoon, squinting slightly in the glare of the battery-powered work light. He looked down at me from the top of the ladder, where he'd been dusting off the chandelier in the foyer of Milkweed Mansion. We'd decided that while the cobwebs and dust were definitely scary, they were also gross, and a more elegant approach to our haunted house might be appreciated here.

"I need to film someone for a dating video in their natural environment. I have to capture them doing stuff they love to do and ask some questions. It's supposed to capture the real person and make them look attractive for this dating app."

He shook his head, and his brow creased. The one-sided light brought out the strong lines of his face and threw a long, film-noir-worthy shadow that extended up and behind him. "I don't need to be on a dating app."

"I'm not saying *you* do. This isn't actually going to be used on the dating app. It's like a prototype thing they can show to investors and prospective customers and get them excited about paying for a high-end video profile."

Landon crossed his arms over his filthy "Trust me I'm a Jedi" T-shirt and lounged at the top of the ladder — something only he could possibly do — while obviously trying not to laugh. "Who the hell would pay for that?"

"I don't know. Egomaniacs? Lonely people? I'm not here to judge. But I need the money, Landon. I really, really need the money. And can you get down here? I'm getting a crick in my neck."

He sighed, put down the cleaning rag next to the bucket at the tippy-top of the ladder, and made his way down.

"What do you want, Kayla?" he asked in a low voice when he reached the floor and stood in front of me. Here, he was only a little taller than I was. Only now, his eyes bored into mine, and his tone carried all kinds of suggestiveness that wasn't there a minute before.

So he hadn't forgotten last night.

God knows I hadn't.

I swallowed and tried to sound confident. "They gave me an impossible deadline." I glanced at his *Star Wars* T-shirt. "Help me, Obi-Wan Kenobi. You're my only hope."

He guffawed. "OK, but only if it doesn't take more than an hour. I have to wrangle the electrician and the plumbers tomorrow."

"A half hour. I swear. We can do a couple of shots at the apartment with your golf clubs, and then — "

"I hate golf." His voice was harder now, and he crossed his arms.

"Um — yeah. Sorry. Maybe with your glove, tossing a softball in the air, looking cute? Because you're on your company's softball team, right?"

"Nice of you to notice." His voice had softened again, and his dark eyes danced. "And you think I'm cute?"

"I — oh, hell. I mean, my friends think you're cute."

He took a step closer, smelling of sweat and cedar and lime, and I tried not to faint.

"What about you?" he asked.

"Landon. *Landon.* I'm asking you this as a professional." Oh, God. I wanted to lick him. "We can do a quick shot at the apartment in the morning, and I'll film you working here now. And then tomorrow here at the mansion we'll do the interview. Twenty minutes, OK?"

"You're not answering my question." His voice was deep and low and sent a sizzle through my veins. "If I have to answer your questions, you have to answer mine."

I looked up into those eyes. "Y-y-yes?"

He hit me with the Fireworks. "Yes what?"

"You're cute?"

"Is that a question?"

"No. I mean, I'm answering your question. So you agree?"

"That I'm cute? I prefer dashing, sexy ... "

"Landon!" Hell, yes, he was all those things.

"Have you considered getting an investor? Then you won't have to do ridiculous video jobs."

"I'm still thinking about it." I huffed in frustration. "Will you do it? Fifteen minutes tomorrow. Just fifteen minutes on camera, and then we're back to the grind."

"Grind." He took another step closer, letting his hands fall to his sides so his chest almost touched mine. "Interesting choice of words."

I blinked up at him like a vole who'd been pulled from its hole. "Are you fucking with me?"

He whispered back, "Only if you want me to."

I stepped back and took a deep breath, shaking off his spell. "Forget it. I'll find someone else. Penelope probably knows some — "

"I'll do it."

"What?"

"I'll do it," he said, his voice retreating from Ludicrous Sexy and returning to Everyday Hot. "Ten minutes?"

"Fifteen, max. Please?"

He smiled, showing the dimples. *Holy shit.* "OK." He started back up the ladder, then called back down to me. "Can you clean up around the kitchen sink so the plumbers can get in there? And make sure they can get to the bathroom plumbing, too?"

"I can do that," I said. But first I got my camera out of its case — I'd grabbed it when I went home to change into my grubby clothes — and got a few shots of him swabbing the crystals in the chandelier. Gently, he washed away the grime on each crystal to reveal their almost liquid shimmer under the bright work light.

I probably filmed him longer than I should have. With the camera as a shield, it was one way of staring at him without actually gawking. Watching him touching each prism, his fingers deft, his attention focused.

Remembering how his hands felt as they slid along my skin.

YOU'D THINK two people who ended up at the same work site each day would go in the same car, but we never did. Landon had his errands to run, and I had mine. Plus, we had another, unstated reason for not car-pooling. If anything, the tension between us had grown to excruciating levels as he'd transformed from annoying roommate to skilled helper to project partner to the object of my drooling lust.

Mostly, I hid the drooling.

In the morning, we met for the interview out by the concrete bench we'd excavated during the garden cleanup.

"So where were you last night?" Landon asked as I set up my tripod, camera and a battery-powered fill light under one of the oak trees with the mansion in the background.

Interesting. Landon wondered where *I* was for a change.

"I had to meet with Cali and Thea about the website, so I got in late. It has to be ready by Friday."

Was that relief I saw in his eyes? "Friday!"

"That's when the press release goes out. Marla's got it all planned. And it'll be ready, though it's putting a lot of pressure on my friends, especially to get the ticket sales set up. They're going to be sold in time blocks, with the VIP tickets separate — two hundred fifty bucks a pop. Is that crazy?"

"Not much for rich people, especially with drinks by the Bohemia Bartenders, Ez's band playing and Jace doing tours. Do you have food planned?"

"Millie says she knows a new caterer who wants to get her name out there and is willing to work for half price." More money out of my pocket, but hopefully advance ticket sales would take care of that and more.

Behind me, the sound of hammering and a boom box filled the air as a crew built the forms for concrete footers for the new gazebo. Look at me, learning terms like "footers." Though I left all the technical stuff to Landon. "I guess I'm going to have to ask them to stop, huh?"

A few minutes later, at my request, the construction crew had jumped in their truck and left on a breakfast run. I'd just clipped the microphone to Landon's collar — I let him run it up under his shirt from the battery pack, though I was dying to do it myself — and I was making last-minute adjustments to the focus.

I slipped on my headphones and eyeballed Landon. He wore jeans, a white button-up shirt with the sleeves rolled up and a skinny black tie, along with black high-tops. I'd asked him to wear something different from his usual work clothes and nearly fainted in pleasure when he appeared in this getup.

I was trying to keep it professional. Really. "Put your foot up on the bench and look casual."

"What am I, a J.C. Penney model?"

"It's better than having you just stand there."

He put his foot up on the bench. Oh dear God, he did look like a model. The move made his jeans cling beautifully to his ass, and his crisp shirt caressed his pecs.

I swallowed more drool. "Say a few words so I can check the sound level."

"A few words."

"Smart-ass. More words than that."

He looked around and assumed a sportscaster voice. "We're standing here outside Milkweed Mansion, about to interview the infamous Landon Putter, well known for his love of choco-late chip cookies."

I laughed and tweaked up his mike's volume. "OK, you sound good. Start out by introducing yourself — your first name and one memorable thing about you. Like for me, it might be, 'Hi, I'm Kayla, and I see the world as one big, beautiful movie.'"

"Do you really?"

"Well, sometimes I see it as more of a Quentin Tarantino movie, but yeah, it's a movie."

He smiled. "Neat. I go to the movies a lot."

"You do?" Another explanation for why he never used to be home much.

"Yeah. We should go sometime. OK. Are you ready?"

I tried not to think about a movie date with Landon and zoomed in, going for a head-and-shoulders shot for the intro-duction. "OK, go."

His eyes locked on the lens, and I pictured a million women swooning. I was one of them. He was looking at *me.* That was the idea. Every single woman looking at him would think the same thing.

He's looking at me.

"Hi," he said, a hint of a smile playing about his lips. His voice had gone lower and more intimate. Damn. It was like warm butterscotch drizzled over brownies spiked with pheromones. "I'm Landon, and the one thing I want out of life is true love."

CHAPTER 17

*L*andon's gaze smoldered for a few more seconds into the lens, and then he looked up at me. "Well?"

"Mmm ... mmhmm," I managed, feeling hot all over. "Yes. That was great. Was that a real answer?"

"Of course." I couldn't tell if he was teasing or not. "Isn't true love what every red-blooded guy wants?"

He was totally teasing. Wasn't he? This was going to be a lot harder than I thought. But I'd promised him this would only take fifteen minutes. I could survive fifteen minutes of Landon wooing the theoretical girl on the other side of the camera, right?

"Fine," I said. "Can you talk about some of the things you do and like to do? Like your job and hobbies and stuff? You can keep it brief."

"That's good, since my hobby is work."

"And softball. And the Sport That Shall Not Be Named for which you need a putter."

"Touché." I zoomed out a little so every delicious inch of him was visible. This time, he addressed the camera in a slightly less sexy tone. "Though I like to play softball, go to the movies and shoot pool with my friends, I'm a builder for a living. I love to renovate old houses and make them feel new again. I believe every house needs TLC to become a home, and every home should be a unique space that's perfect for the people who live in it. Kind of the way everyone needs someone who's perfect for them."

"Holy bucking seahorses," I mumbled.

"What?"

"That's fantastic," I said more loudly. We couldn't let this dating video get out. Every woman in Florida would want to bang Landon's hammer. "Can you talk about the kind of dates you like to go on?"

He nodded, looking thoughtful for a moment as I zoomed in a bit. "I like dates that are either comfortable or adventurous. It's fun to do something your date really loves to do and see her in an environment where she's relaxed and happy. And after you get to know each other a little bit, it's a thrill to take an adventure with her. That doesn't mean jumping out of a plane, though it could. It really means trying something new. An adventure of discovery. If you're compatible with someone, you're happy doing a cozy night at home or an adventure. The important thing is that you're with someone you care about."

I was now thoroughly jealous of anyone who'd ever gone on a date with Landon.

"That was really good." Understatement of the year. "Let's just do one more question. What are you looking for in a life partner?"

"This is assuming I want a life partner," he joked.

"Humor me. It's for the video."

"Can I put my leg down now?"

"Why don't you sit on the bench? I'll get a close-up shot for this one."

He lowered his leg, did a couple of quick stretches and sat on the bench, leaning forward so his elbows were on his knees. He clasped his hands in front of him, looking as earnest as I'd ever seen him. I was starting to think Landon had missed his calling. He should've been an actor or a pitchman.

"Will this work?" he asked.

"Definitely. Let me adjust a few things here." I lowered the tripod a little and zoomed in so the camera was framed on his face, like it was having an intimate conversation with him.

"What was the question again?" he asked.

"Very funny. The question is: What are you looking for in a life partner?"

The subtlest of smiles touched his lips as he gazed into the camera. "It's hard to think about forever in today's world, but I think it's possible to find the right person and make forever happen. For me, she's smart. She thinks about things, but she also likes to have fun. She doesn't take everything seriously. She understands what it means to live in the moment. She takes risks, but not stupid ones. She's a good friend as much as she's sexy — with the total understanding that sexy is something that is as much a part of that light inside her as it is her smile or the confident way she carries herself. She supports my plans but has her own dreams and ideas, and I love her for it. That's the woman I want forever."

For a moment, I let the video roll as he looked into the lens. I almost forgot the camera was there. With him talking right into my ears through the headphones, speaking to me — thanks to the beautiful illusion of the camera — I was completely lost. Finally, I dimly registered the sound of the wind and distant cars and reluctantly hit the stop button. I pulled off my headphones. "How do you do that?"

"What?"

"Just 'turn on' for the camera. It's a gift."

"I took a public speaking class once, and one tip I took away is that it helps sometimes to pick out an audience of one. Talk to that person, and whatever you're saying will feel natural." His dark eyes seemed to sparkle in the dappled sunlight, but he wasn't joking this time. "I was talking to you."

I was transfixed. Speechless. *He was talking to me?* And then a blast of salsa music and the crunching of tires on the driveway heralded the return of the construction crew.

"Thanks," was all I eked out before he grinned, pulled off his tie and microphone, handed me the gear and wandered over to see where the crew stood. The cement truck was coming that afternoon.

In my head, I was going over what he'd said. *I was talking to you.* Of course, he meant I was a safe audience, that audience of one he imagined to keep from being nervous on camera. Not that I was thoughtful and smart and sexy and confident and a good friend, too ...

Was I? Could I be?

Maybe I didn't think the jerk in Orlando would be mine forever, but I'd been open to the idea — probably because I was completely naive, imagining us growing from the lame kids' show to a Hollywood power couple, making great TV and movies. From the very first time he blew off one of my ideas, I should have known he'd never respect me, that he was only using me. But sometimes it takes a while to admit you're wrong, to realize that all those feelings that come with sex might have nothing to do with love. And then you crawl back home and get a crappy job and wonder how you can ever feel fresh and smart and alive again. How you can ever take the "closed" sign off your heart.

As I packed up the camera gear, I snuck glances over at Landon chatting with the guys. In Spanish. He had more layers than an onion.

The thing is, no matter how sweet they are, onions can make you cry.

$\mathcal{T}$ime started to accelerate at Milkweed Mansion. Things happened fast because they had to. It took a week of intense work, but the electrician and his crew updated all the wiring in the house. He said there were some lights in the second-floor corridors that appeared to have wiring that went nowhere, but he got them hooked up, too, and an inspection led us to have that most precious of things, electricity. Air-conditioning would come later, but Landon brought in some big hurricane-level fans, and finally the Florida heat was losing its edge — about all we could ask of early fall.

The plumbers had good news and bad news. The good news was that the pipes had been replaced in the 1950s and were copper, in pretty good shape. The bad news was that one of the pipes upstairs had a leak that we found the hard way, when the water was turned on and it started "raining" in the kitchen.

At least it wasn't the library, I kept telling myself.

As the dates for our fundraiser neared, we got a working sink in the kitchen and a working bathroom downstairs. There would be tons more to do, including complete overhauls of the upstairs bathrooms, but none of that had to happen before the haunted house. In fact, the crappier the rooms looked, the better they served our haunting needs.

There was soon a parade of artists through the house, chattering about what they would do with each room. I let Millie wrangle them and gave them the freedom to come up with whatever scenes they wanted, though I did go down the list just to make sure there wasn't anything that would result in vomiting patrons. With Cali's brother Damien, you never knew. His multimedia sculptures could be downright disturbing.

He and Penelope worked together on the concept for the outdoor sculpture. When I'd suggested they use the big oak stump as a base, Damien came up with the creepy framework for a wraith with a demented skull face and skeletal hands.

Penelope, the costume designer, created an ethereal, tattered robe for it. It had a base of gauzy white fabric layered with translucent orange and purple and strips of black, as well as a hood. Her lighting designer friend Alan came up with shifting special-effects lights in purple and orange and blacklight spotlights that made it glow. I had to admit, when they got it in place a couple of weeks before the VIP party and I saw it luminous and swaying in the breeze at night, I found it unnerving. It was beautiful and sinister at the same time, partly because it was so large — it must have been over twenty feet tall. Traffic slowed down on the river road to look at it, and within three days of it going up, ticket sales tripled.

Work crews were in and out, many of them donating time and material, but my bank account continued to dwindle. I had to nag Rick to pay me promptly for the Landon video, which he raved about. He even asked if Landon might do a commercial later on.

Landon laughed when I told him. "I did that just for you," he said with a wink. So maybe it had all been a lark, but I still kept thinking about everything he'd said in the video.

We'd reached a delicate balance working together, though whenever we got into a tight spot in the house, like when I had to hold something in place while he screwed it — you know, with a screwdriver and screws, though I was definitely thinking of something else — my body still dinged like a pinball machine. I wasn't sure how he'd worked his way into my blood, but he made it simmer with every joke and gesture.

For his part, he seemed more considerate than ever, jumping to my aid whenever I needed help, to the point where I wondered if the ghost had killed the old Landon and replaced him with this perfect man who would transform into a monster and eat me in my sleep.

I might've had a few fantasies about him eating me in my sleep, if you know what I mean.

But at night, he'd gone back to finding things to do out of the house or watching sports.

One rare night when he was in, he turned on TCM, and we ended up watching *The Maltese Falcon* together. We had a great time quoting the quotable lines and commenting on the characters. It was probably my favorite Bogart movie, and it did weird things to my insides that Landon was as into it as I was. So he *did* like movies, and that was just one more reason to like him.

Still, I had the impression that outside of our renovation work, he might've been avoiding me. This weird hot and cold thing was happening. While the sexual tension ramped up like an action sequence in a Spielberg film, Landon became more polite and distant.

Maybe his obvious stepping back should've made me cool my jets, but it had the opposite effect. I was ready to launch whenever I saw him.

I focused on learning more about the house in the slim free time I had between the hard physical work we were doing and bedtime. The entries in Flora's journal started simply enough, but soon it was about much more than roses and pineapples.

"While I snip and dig in the garden with my roses," Flora Fountain wrote, "Stanford whiles away the hours in his workshop, inventing all manner of solutions in search of a problem. Last week, he created a pulley system to haul our trunks up to the second floor through the windows, though it is unclear if we will need them again. It is unlikely I will ever go back to New York. The warmth here is so much better for my lungs. Between his physical labor and my scandalous sunburn, the servants think we're mad. But with no children to dote upon, we need our little baby projects."

When the historical society's Ken Motebarkle made a surprise visit on the day the new gazebo was being delivered, I was almost glad to see him. We chatted on the porch. I had a lot of questions about the house, but first I wanted to assure the tall, thin, graying historian, who made me think of Ichabod Crane, that we were doing everything we could to preserve the character of the mansion.

"But that's new. Why didn't you save the old gazebo?" He adjusted his glasses and stared at the noisy, beeping truck backing up to the gazebo zone with its unwieldy cargo.

The new octagonal gazebo was gorgeous, painted white with a tiny cupola atop the shingled roof. The cupola had a copper roof and a finial. This donation was assured with its own small plaque on the structure, since it was a great advertisement for the builder. Another crew was already working on stone steps for it and a paver patio that would make it a striking centerpiece of the yard.

"I love it," I told the historian. "The old one was a safety hazard and beyond restoration."

"Are you sure? Did you have an expert look at it?"

"If you mean a historian, no. If you mean an expert in construction, yes — Landon Putter, the manager of this project."

"From Putter Homes? You mean the fellow over there directing traffic?"

Landon was now standing near the truck, gesturing so it would be perfectly lined up to tilt the bed and slide the gazebo in place. A handful of burly guys stood ready to guide it.

"That's him," I said.

"His company is a prime player in destroying the character of this area. What can he possibly know?" Motebarkle said with disdain.

"A hell of a lot," I said with unexpected vehemence. "He's a specialist in old houses." Or at least he wanted to be. "You should see what he's doing with the place inside."

"Hmph. Actually, yes, I would like to see what you're doing inside."

Worrying I'd overpromised, I opened the front door for him. It still had plywood over the center of it, and someone had spray-painted "KEEP OUT" on it in the spirit of the haunted house. "We've barely started, but that's why we're having the fundraiser."

"Ah, yes, the haunted house," he said dismissively. "You couldn't do anything more dignified?"

"There's a VIP party. That'll be dignified." I really sounded defensive now. "Besides, how many high teas would we need to bring in the kind of money it's going to take to get this house renovated?"

Ken looked at me over his glasses. "Your little event is not going to do it either."

"We'll see," I said as diplomatically as I could, but I was fuming, especially because I knew he was probably right.

I gave him a very brief tour of the house, having to usher him along as he hungrily took in details. "I should have brought my camera," he muttered, and I assured him that we were documenting everything. He got more excited as we went along. The ballroom reflected a great deal of work already, with new-to-us chandeliers I'd found in an antique store in town, and the library had him almost giddy.

I didn't tell him about the secret closet. I didn't want him to know just yet. It was weird, but I felt like that was something for me. And Landon. Maybe our friends, too, but you get the idea.

However, I did show him the ledgers, which were still on the library table. "You might find these interesting."

Ken exclaimed over the mundane entries as if they were a lost folio of Shakespeare's. "And look," he said when he got to where the handwriting changed. "This is where Stanford started taking over the records, I bet."

"Why?"

Ken straightened and looked at me as if I had three heads. "You didn't know? Flora Fountain died of tuberculosis just a few years after they moved here."

I gasped. "Her journal says something about the weather being good for her health — "

"You have her journal?" Ken exclaimed. "I must see it."

"I — it's at home. It's really just a gardening record." I was underplaying it a little, but I wanted to keep it until I'd read the whole thing.

"I don't think you realize what you have here," he said, his impatience showing. "This house is a treasure — "

"So everyone keeps telling me."

" — and it's one of Bohemia's last links to its founders."

"Mr. Motebarkle? I get it. Trust me, I get it. But the house is mine now. I will share the journal with you in time, and you and others will be able to experience the house when it's ready for visitors. Would you like a ticket to the VIP party?" I asked as an afterthought.

"Certainly not," he said. "But I expect an invitation once these silly theatrics are over so I can do more research."

I tried hard not to roll my eyes. "I bet the ghost doesn't think they're silly."

"Please. You don't actually believe that rubbish."

The house sighed, as was its wont, and a strange fluttering noise emanated from its heart. I really had come to believe it had a heart.

Ken looked around sharply, then "hmphed" again and headed for the door. On the porch, he shook my hand briefly and departed without another word.

I looked over at the workers in the yard. Landon smiled and waved, then did a game-show gesture to indicate the white gazebo, now neatly in place.

I chuckled and gave him a thumbs-up, feeling strangely grateful for this man and this adventure. For the river and the sky. For the gazebo and its promise of music and weddings and life, as I wondered which roses might look best planted next to it.

CHAPTER 19

*I*t was Thursday. Our VIP opening was Friday. And Milkweed Mansion was in utter chaos.

Landon was directing various crews to clean up their work and stow supplies in a surprisingly attractive shed he'd stuck in the corner of the property. It was in the same style as the gazebo.

"A gift from my dad," he said. "We need someplace to store stuff while the renovation is happening. You can get rid of it later if you want."

"Are you kidding? I might have to live in there," I said.

"What, and leave our glamorous apartment?"

I laughed, but that got me to thinking. No matter how this turned out, I probably would leave his apartment. I couldn't deal with his polite distance when I just wanted to kiss him all over, and I knew I shouldn't kiss him all over because of my disastrous history with men. Or man. One man who had destroyed my faith in the rest of them.

Anyway, the shed was starting to look like a good idea.

My artist friends were almost done setting up their scenes in the mansion, and they agreed to give Landon and I a run-through once the sun went down.

"Penelope says it will look stupid in daylight," Millie told me as she went through one of her checklists as we stood on the porch. "And Alex picked up the tab for the caterer for Friday."

"Wait. What? I didn't ask him to do that." Did this mean he was officially an investor now? Because I hadn't decided on bringing in a partner yet. I wanted to see how the fundraiser did.

"He says since the art museum is technically a co-sponsor, it was the least he could do. Trust me, Kayla, he wants to do this. He's thrilled this place is finally getting some TLC."

I bit my lip and tried to push my anxiety back down into my gut, where I kept it with the leftover pizza and excessive amounts of iced tea. I had to admit, I felt a tiny bit of relief, too. That bill was going to hurt. "OK. How are VIP ticket sales doing?"

"When we announced the famous *Jace Edison* would be leading the tours for the VIP night, they jumped. We are very close to selling out. And he's agreed to have his photo taken with guests for an extra donation."

"What a great idea!"

"I'll be buying one of those for sure," Millie said.

I giggled. "He *is* the hottest thing since tiki torches."

"Talking about me again?" came a voice behind me. It was Landon, coming up the porch steps, shooting the Fireworks at both of us. Was it me, or did he look happier since we started this project? He was finally doing the kind of renovation work he loved. But I couldn't take advantage of his love for the work once the fundraiser was over. He had a job to go back to, and I had some decisions to make about how to move forward.

"We're talking about Jace," Millie said. "He'll be leading the VIP haunted tour, and he'll do the run-through tonight with you guys."

"Excellent," he said. "And I'm treating all of you to a round of drinks at The Junction Box afterward."

"You can't do that!" I exclaimed.

He raised an eyebrow. "Why not?"

"Because this is my project. I mean, it's my house. You're the man when it comes to the project, but this is my responsibility. I'll buy the drinks."

"Don't be silly. You can't afford to buy a seltzer water at this point."

Ouch. The truth hurt.

He saw my expression and his Fireworks vanished. "I'm sorry, Kayla. I didn't mean anything by that. I'm having a great time, you know." Millie quietly slipped into the house as he continued. "I can afford it. It's no more than I would've spent on a night out any time before this project started."

"You don't know how these people drink."

He laughed. "That's why I said one round. Are you OK? Do you really mind?"

My eyes felt weirdly wet, and my nose prickled. "I — I don't mind. It's just that I feel responsible. I feel like I should be doing this by myself, and yet everyone is being so nice and helpful. And you — my God, Landon, you've given up your whole life for this project."

He looked down at me with those sweet brown eyes, soft and warm now. "I haven't given up anything."

I found myself leaning subtly toward him, and he gently grasped my arm, pulling me closer.

A horrific scream from inside the house jerked us apart, and we dashed through the door and up the stairs toward the sound. Then up one more flight to the tower, since no one seemed to be lingering on the second floor.

Duncan and Thea were sticking their tongues down each other's throats in the tower room amid a spaghetti tangle of dangling white paper cutouts, gauze and crepe paper.

"What the hell?" Landon exclaimed.

They pulled apart and had the grace to look embarrassed.

Thea cleared her throat. "Sorry. I was just practicing."

"And I was coming to her rescue," Duncan said. "I can't resist a lass in distress."

I snorted a laugh.

"Neither can I," Landon said dryly, and I elbowed him because I knew he was talking about me. I had been in distress, and he'd come to my rescue. But soon we'd leave phase one of the crisis and go into phase two — long-term plans. And I was pretty sure there wasn't room for me in his.

Or room for him in mine?

"I hope we didn't ruin the surprise," I said. The artists had been keeping us out of most of the rooms for a couple of days while they set everything up.

"For this room?" Thea's smile was smug, and her deep blue eyes shone. "Oh, no. It's going to look completely different at night."

"I can't wait." And I meant it. I had bats fluttering around in my stomach. This was going to be cool.

It had to be.

CHAPTER 20

*L*andon and I went back home to shower (separately, alas) and change into clean but casual clothes for our preview of the haunted house. We both ended up in jeans and black T-shirts — his with a jack-o'-lantern on it that said "I'm just here for the boos," and mine a plain V-neck that did amazing things for my cleavage. Judging from the quick scan he gave me, I'm pretty sure he noticed.

Why was I tormenting him? Or, more to the point, why was I torturing myself?

We decided to car-pool for once, and he volunteered to drive. We climbed into his truck, and he flicked on the radio. "That historian's show is supposed to be on."

"Oh yeah," I said. "Marla said Motebarkle was going to talk about the mansion."

The twenty-minute segment perfectly filled the drive time. And what started out happily — with a brief mention that the house was being reopened and an interesting history of the mansion and the family — ended in a nightmare.

"Alas, the new owner of the Fountain house" — he didn't call it Milkweed Mansion except for one dismissive mention of its "unfortunate nickname" — "is sullying its hallowed halls with a Halloween haunted house. This event is a smack in the face to the family, or I'm sure it *would* be if any of the descendants still lived. Especially given the baseless rumors of the house being haunted. I only hope this precious legacy of Bohemia's early history isn't destroyed by this callous money grab when, by all rights, it should be converted into a historical museum."

I slammed my fist against the truck door as the segment ended.

"Hey!" Landon switched off the radio. "Take it easy!"

"'By all rights'? I own the place. And 'money grab' is a complete joke. Money pit is more like it."

"You do know Motebarkle has been begging the city council for money to expand the historical museum for years? It gets under his skin that the city is supporting your plans for the house."

"It's not like they've approved a grant yet. They're giving us some nice PR and fast permitting, maybe."

"Believe me, that's huge," Landon said. "Don't let it get to you. Your plan will respect the history of the house and will allow controlled public access. You could even have an open house once in a while, maybe in conjunction with the historical society."

"The last thing I want to do is work with that guy! And what if the city decides to shut us down after that little diatribe?"

"Don't worry about it. They've clearly demonstrated their support for you. Give the haters a little time to appreciate what you're doing. One thing you learn in construction is patience."

"At this point, I'm more worried about Motebarkle tanking my ticket sales."

Landon flashed me a brief Fireworks smile. "Wait and see."

He pulled into the drive of Milkweed Mansion and parked among the other cars under the trees. We were working with a nearby office building to offer event parking and a shuttle once we opened Friday, but these were all our friends. I was nervous and excited to see what they'd wrought.

Darkness was just settling in, and the gauzy creature atop the tree stump, the huge skeletal wraith, was shifting in the breeze, looming over us as we walked up to the porch.

"Damn if that thing doesn't look alive," I said.

"Maybe you should leave it there after the haunted house."

"Ha. Oh, look. It's Jace. I think."

An elegant vampire awaited us on the front porch. *Damn.* Lean, tall, dark-haired and impossibly handsome, Jace in vampire garb was enough to make me want to offer up my neck for immortality. Penelope had won the boyfriend lottery with this one.

"Welcome, my friends. Would you care for a drink before you go in?" He offered us a metal goblet that looked like it was brimming with blood.

"Um, yuck?" I said.

"I'll try it," Landon said, and I stared open-mouthed as he drank from the goblet. "Mmm, cranberry juice."

"Are you going to do that at showtime?" I asked Jace.

He grinned. "We'll have disposable cups, but I wanted you to get the best impression." Then he stood taller, sweeping his cape over his shoulder, and assumed his character with a sultry voice. "I understand the Realtor sent you. In the market for a haunted house?"

I laughed. "Absolutely."

"Then come right this way."

The chandelier in the foyer was dimly lit and complemented by undulating colored lights. My own anticipation worked against me here. Nothing chased us, but the general decay of the space increased my sense of dread, especially with the weird sounds coming from the rest of the house — pounding music. Moans?

I glanced at Landon, whose eyebrows were raised at the ambience.

"Perhaps you'd like to see the parlor," Jace purred as he took us that way.

In the as yet untouched parlor, furniture was covered with blood-spattered sheets under dim, undulating, atmospheric lighting, as if a murder scene was frozen in time. And then one of the "chairs" leapt up at us — a person covered in one of the bloody cloths. We both jumped, with me grabbing Landon in an embarrassing display of terror.

"Nice," I muttered.

"Thanks," came Wyatt's muffled voice. "By the way, Cali took pictures already."

"Thanks," I said, and couldn't help a giggle. It was hard to have a conversation with a bloody sheet.

We skipped the kitchen, which, while not renovated yet, would be used to stage provisions for the party and a small concession during the rest of the tours. The dining room was next, and it was amazing. "Floating" candles (battery-operated LEDs, my analytical mind determined) hung above a cloth-covered table covered with all manner of disgusting dishes, including a "body" with its innards spilling out. Skeletons and a couple of costumed ghouls were eating the macabre feast, and there were a lot of squishy sounds in the background that enhanced the queasy scene.

In the middle of the table was one of those chocolate fountains, only this looked like it was gushing with blood. One of the ghouls stood and moved closer, sweeping a finger through the liquid and holding it out to us. "Want a taste?" he asked in a low, gravelly voice.

This time, Landon said no, and we threw ourselves back

when the ghoul stuck the finger in our faces and screamed, "We're starving!"

"Not so scary so far," I whispered as we got into the hallway. "I didn't recognize those guys, but maybe it was the makeup."

"We brought in a few of our friends from the Chamberlain Theater," Jace whispered back, then resumed his vampiric tour guide persona. "I think you'll appreciate the number of bedrooms we have here at the mansion. It's very restful." He led us up the stairs, where framed holographic photos were hung along the walls, lit just right so they seemed to be staring at us as they changed from grim-faced humans to rotten-faced creeps.

The music was getting louder, some sort of grinding, screaming metal that grated on my ears. I liked to rock out, but this was unnerving, partly because there was also a soundtrack, real or recorded, of yowling and moaning and crying layered under the death metal.

"The nursery has been decorated in such a charming way," Jace said, showing us to the first bedroom on the long corridor.

A broken-down crib was off to one side, with a mobile hanging above it consisting of creepy dolls with eyes missing, a meat cleaver, a bloody rattle and more. Tiny coffins were stacked in another corner. With her back to us, a woman was cooing over what must have been a baby, rocking the child in her arms.

Then the woman turned toward us. Her hair was a fright (a wig?), her dress was tattered, her feet bare, and through the magic of makeup, it looked as if her eyes had been ripped out.

"Fuck," Landon said under his breath.

The woman held out the baby toward us, and I realized that it had a bloody stump where its head was supposed to be. "Have you seen my baby's head?" she asked in a creaky voice, and I belatedly realized it was Sloane holding the desecrated doll.

Jace guided us out the door. "That's just *disturbing*," I whispered.

"Well, that is the idea of a haunted house," Landon said.

In the bedroom across the hall, glowing, translucent specters spun slowly. I realized they were made of chicken wire and gauze and painted with something that shone a whitish green under the blacklight. Fog rolled across the floor of the small room, and sinister sounds played from somewhere, just audible above the increasingly loud rock music. In my homeowner brain, I remembered this ceiling needed a lot of work, so a few hooks didn't bother me, especially when the ghosts looked so cool.

In the next gloomy bedroom, piles of "bodies" littered the floor. The forms were wrapped in garbage bags and duct tape. At the center of the room was a person in a wheelchair, hunched over, moaning. "Can you help me?" came an old-woman voice. "Just come a little closer."

"I'm not coming closer," I said.

Landon laughed and took a couple of steps into the room, and then the figure in the wheelchair reared up with a baseball bat, screaming bloody murder.

This time we almost knocked Jace over trying to get out of the room.

"Was that Bennett?" Landon asked as we took a second to gather ourselves.

"Yeah, I think so." I sucked in a few more breaths, then gestured to Jace to continue. "Maybe we should warn people with heart conditions against doing the tour."

"Good idea," Landon said.

The music was getting louder, but there was another sound now. Crying. A child crying.

"We had to send this child to bed without any supper, but you can see how well taken care of he is," Jace said, gesturing to the door. This was the door that already had a hole in it, just about at eye level, so we peered through the ragged gap.

When we looked in, in the middle of the broken bed was what appeared to be a child rocking himself, facing away from us. The crying sound was the sort of thing that crept into your soul. That was sinister enough, but the child was completely surrounded by ghastly skeletons in shifting, mostly blood-red lighting.

"Realistic, isn't it?" Jace asked.

"What *is* that?" I responded.

"Damien's invention. Some sort of robotic movement. Pretty freaky, right?" Then Jace assumed his smooth, low tour-guide voice again. "This way, if you please."

Past the bathroom, which had crime-scene tape over the open door and a lot of fake blood scattered around, was the last bedroom on this hallway. Jace gently pushed us inside, where the deafening music radiating from an old-school boom box was enough to rattle anyone. There were two punked-out, scary-looking dudes spray-painting the walls. There was graffiti every-where, a lot of it pretty morbid shit, and the colorful walls were glowing wildly in the blacklight. But it was pure art, too.

The rational homeowner voice in my head reminded me it would all be repainted, and the floor was covered in plastic. The irrational voice was shaken up by the extremely loud music and the erratic movements of the punks, who seemingly hadn't noticed us.

Just then, one of them whipped around and charged us.

"What the hell are you doing in here?" he yelled — Cali's brother Damien, I realized — and then he sprayed his can of paint right in our faces!

We yelled and stumbled out of the room before we realized we'd been spritzed with water, and then we had to laugh.

And then we heard Damien laughing and telling his friend — Gary, I was pretty sure — "I told you it would be awesome, man."

Jace chuckled, too, as he led us to the other hallway, where the master bedroom was located. He opened the door to the room. A dark curtain had been set up just inside the entrance. "We have a spirit guide to lead you through," he said. "You must hold hands." And then a gloved hand stuck out from the other side of the curtain and beckoned.

I shot a look at Landon. He smiled and nodded. I grasped the hand, and Landon grabbed my other hand. Then we were being pulled through an almost entirely dark room, touched by all kinds of weird things, including hands that brushed my arms and shoulders. I kept twitching and startling and yelping and wanting to brush stuff away from my face, but with both hands captured, I could only follow. Besides, our spirit guide kept saying in a soft, feminine voice, "If you let go, you are lost." That alone was eerie as hell. Landon squeezed my hand, a warm and steady comfort in the disembodiment of the dark room, until the figure led us back to the entrance and gently pushed us into the hallway.

"That was weird," I said a little breathlessly. Landon was still holding my hand. He gave it another squeeze before letting go. When I glanced at his face, he had a strangely serious expression. "Were you scared?" I asked him.

"Terrified," he answered, a hint of humor in his tone.

Maybe he was joking about being scared, but he was definitely thoughtful.

Jace bestowed us with a sinister look and that horror-show voice.

"The tower awaits, my friends."

CHAPTER 21

*J*ace guided us slowly up the spiral staircase. On the curving steps, trippy, moving lights made the short climb surreal, and then we popped up in the tower room, where unsettling music played in the background. But music wasn't what made this room amazing.

"Wow," I breathed.

White paper cutouts dangled all over the faceted round room, hinting at layers of spiderwebs. Thea, a paper artist, was no doubt behind this design. The beautifully cut paper webs were enhanced by string and strips of gauze hanging from the ceiling and crisscrossing the space. All of this white material was lit up by blacklights, making it all glow intensely blue-purple.

From behind the layers emerged a glowing fluorescent spider. That's right, a multicolored spider — Duncan dressed up with extra legs and crazy glasses that made him look like he had bugged-out mirror eyes.

I realized that in the middle of all the webs, Thea herself was laid out on a chaise lounge. She looked like a virgin sacrifice. While her curly red hair was loose and long, she was dressed all in white, with her hands folded over her chest, so she glowed, too.

Duncan approached her, ominous with all his legs. In two of them — his hands — he held a dagger high above her chest, poised to strike. And then her eyes flew open, she sat straight up, and she screamed that demon-raising scream.

I couldn't help it. I screamed, too. Then Landon and Duncan started laughing, and Thea grinned.

"I told you it would be a surprise," she said.

Jace took us down the back staircase. "The library is the last stop on our little tour," he said. "The librarian loves visitors."

The library was very dimly lit with fake candelabras, and scattered all around us were stacks of books much taller than we were, corkscrewing toward the ceiling in ways that defied physics. They looked like they could fall over at any minute. With a quick glance, I was assured they hadn't been taken from the mansion's shelves.

"How are those supported?" I murmured to Landon.

"Some kind of bendy pole stuck up through them, I think," he murmured back, and then a violent "SHHHH!" drew our attention to the library table.

There, a ghostly librarian — Penelope, I realized, dressed in greenish-white with matching makeup, all aglow — was holding a finger to her lips.

"Your books are overdue," she intoned in a chilling voice. "Come here and pay the fine."

I hadn't been a very good sport with all these beckoning spirits, so I took a tentative step forward.

And then the stacks of books began to fall over right on top of us.

I screamed and jumped back, was actually pulled back by Landon, and then we saw the three main stacks, while leaning *really* far over, weren't going anywhere. They slowly resumed their erect position, thanks to a cable system controlled by a few people I finally saw hiding beneath and behind the furniture.

The ghostly librarian took a step toward us as we chuckled.

"Thank you for freaking us out," I told her.

And then she yanked an ax from behind her and screamed, "I TOLD YOU TO BE QUIET!"

I almost ejected from my Skechers as I screamed in answer, and Jace was laughing as he pulled us out of the room. Landon was grinning, too.

"Oh, shut up," I said, but then I had to smile back. "That was pretty great."

"It's my favorite," Jace said, back in his Jace voice. "Damien again. He has a gift for mechanicals. And of course Penelope is *stunning.*"

With Penelope's screech, the various ghouls began materializing in the foyer as themselves, turning off music and lights, stripping off costumes, laughing and going over what they'd done and what they could do better for the VIP opening the next night.

"I'm just looking forward to doing my vlog in that crazy spider outfit," Duncan said.

"You all are completely fantastic," I gushed. "How can I ever thank you enough?"

"Alcohol?" Damien said.

"Millie told you, right? First round on me at The Junction Box," Landon said.

As everyone scrambled to get back into their civilian clothes and shut down the theatrics, I looked at Landon. "What do you think?"

"It's really awesome. Once word gets out about this weekend, next weekend's ticket sales are a lock."

"Will it be enough?"

He shrugged and smiled. "It will be a good start. And then you have decisions to make."

"I know. An investment partner. The thing is, I don't want to go into a partnership only being able to pay for a tiny fraction of the renovation. That's basically giving up all control to someone else."

"Come here. Turn around." He laid his hands on my shoulders and began digging into them with those magical hands, massaging all the tension out of my muscles. I flashed back to those moments we had on our couch. Lightning bolts shot from his fingers right to my lady parts. "Don't worry," he was saying. "We'll make money from this. Maybe we'll make money some other way. Business loans are always a possibility. And a good investor will make everything easier."

I sighed and relaxed into his touch. "You're right. No sense in worrying about step one hundred when we're only at step three."

"Exactly." He gave my shoulders one last squeeze, then leaned in and kissed my cheek dangerously close to my neck, where all the little nerve endings sat up and tingled.

I sighed again, and when I turned to look at him, he was giving me the Fireworks.

A FEW HOURS LATER, mixologist Neil's Mai Tais at The Junction Box had made most of the ghouls extremely happy. I was new to tiki drinks, and I could barely sit up straight. But I was as giddy as the others, and my inhibitions had made a run for the border.

"You OK?" Landon asked. He'd been drinking beer and seemed sober.

I leaned my head against his shoulder and smiled up at him. "I feel really good."

Fireworks! Ah, that smile. "Glad to hear it. You should drink some water."

"Always taking care of me. Why are you taking care of me?"

"It's fun."

"Oh, you and your fun," I said, but I took a sip of water, followed by another sip of Mai Tai. My thick paper straw rattled the last ice in the bottom of the glass, and I frowned. "It's gone! I need another one!"

"Are you sure? You have a big day tomorrow."

"Oh, please, Landony *Wann*-doe-neeeee."

He busted out laughing. "I've never seen you like this. Except maybe that time with the banjo."

"Because I hardly ever get drunk, because then I would lose control, and then I might do something stupid where men are concerned." I bit my lip, and his eyes flared.

Just then, as Ez finished playing an impromptu sing-along version of "Bohemian Rhapsody" that had everyone in the bar howling, Jace stood up and addressed our party.

"Why don't we go back to our house for a swim?"

I must've looked puzzled, because Penelope took pity on me and explained. "We bought a house on the beach. Did I not tell you? It's pretty sweet."

"It's fantastic," Jace said. "It has a big pool with a view of the ocean. Laps every morning. Which is why I look like *this*," he joked, winking at me.

I damn near fainted.

"Skinny dipping!" Damien shouted. I wondered if he realized his spiky dark hair and eye makeup were both likely to fail if he went swimming.

There was wide agreement on the beach house, if not naked swimming,

Landon said he was sober enough to drive, and Millie was able to take Bennett and a couple of the others, as was Alex, who'd met us at the bar and drove a big SUV. The rest grabbed an Uber van for the quick trip over to Bohemia Beach.

Landon helped me out of the truck. Even though I felt like I was floating, I was pretty sure I would float right onto my face if I tried to make that big step on my own.

"Hey, isn't this just down the road from your old beach house, Gary?" someone asked.

"Yeah, it's just north of here. The art school owns it now," Gary said. "Though Ez and I have been to this place, before Jace and Pen bought it." He and Ez exchanged a sly glance that was too hot to handle, and I decided not to ask.

A few minutes later, folks had tumbled out to the screened-in lagoon-shaped pool. Music thumped out of the speakers, and Jace was pulling out all manner of beer and wine from behind the bar in the fancy outdoor kitchen and mixing up classic cocktails. "We added some enhancements to this place before we moved in. I love this bar."

The movie star was in his element, and a few people were stripping to their underwear to take a dip. One couple got into the hot tub, which featured a waterfall that flowed into the pool. No one was naked yet, and Damien had passed out on a lounge chair.

"I want to walk on the beach," I said to Landon. I was still buzzed and clung to his arm for support. It couldn't have been because he felt so big and strong and warm. "I never get to walk on the beach."

"Because you're always working."

"Look who's talking!"

"Hey, I'm not arguing with you. Let's walk on the beach."

"Should've worn shorts. These jeans are going to get wet." Hell, they were getting wet already, but not from the waves.

"Roll 'em up," he said.

"Are you laughing at me?"

His eyes were sparkling, and he was covering his mouth with his hands. "No," he mumbled into his hand, but his chest was shaking.

"You're terrible. You roll up your jeans. I'm taking mine off."

OK, so one part of my mind was saying *Kayla, what the hell?* And *don't ever drink Mai Tais again,* while another part was getting all frisky and bold and loved hanging out with this spontaneous crowd. What was one more person in their underwear?

I slipped off my jeans and left them with my shoes by the side of the pool while Landon's eyes got wider. Here's the thing. My shirt was pretty long, so it almost covered my butt anyway. And I had cotton bikini briefs on. I was not a thong kinda girl. Still, I couldn't help noticing the way he scanned me, and suddenly I was buzzed on more than the drinks.

He left his tennis shoes by the pool, too, and rolled up his jeans, and then we took the walkway and steps over the dune out to the dark beach. Everyone's lights were down so as not to disturb any nesting or hatching sea turtles, and it was pretty quiet. No one around. The breeze lifted my hair and rippled my clothes, and for the first time in a long time, I was really — happy.

I looked down, puzzled. Something was different. Then, through my tipsy haze, I realized Landon had ahold of my hand. I was walking hand in hand with Landon. I looked up at him in wonder. He was silent as we walked along to the now distant sound of our friends' party, the hiss of the waves keeping us company.

"Landon?" I whispered.

He paused and looked down at me with a little smile. More of a spark than fireworks. "You OK?"

"I feel really good." I pulled him closer to the dune line, in the shadow of the grassy bank, where it felt more private. I let go of his hand, and then I slipped both of my arms around his waist and gave him a little tug so he was snug against me.

He stood still for a moment, very still, as if he was deciding something, and then he threaded his fingers through my hair, brought me closer and kissed me.

Oh my God. Why had I pushed him away the other night? There were Reasons. There were always Reasons. But now I opened to him without reservation, all my walls dissolving into sparkling butterflies and flying away into the night.

His tongue found mine, and heat blossomed between my legs and all over my body as his hands roamed down my back and cupped my ass through the boring cotton underwear. He kneaded me there, a whole new place to massage, and I gripped him more tightly, crushing myself against his pelvis, feeling the hard bulge there, wanting to know what he'd feel like inside me.

His mouth moved to my neck, tonguing behind my ear, working his way down to the V in my T-shirt. He stretched the fabric with his hand so he could kiss the smooth mounds of flesh above my bra, and I breathed in sharply.

"Take it off," I whispered, and without hesitation, he swept the cotton shirt over my head and tossed it to the sand next to us.

"Kayla." He cupped my breasts through my black lace bra — my bra was *not* boring — and looked into my eyes, searching. "Are you — do you — "

"I'm sure." I licked my lips. "I want you."

CHAPTER 22

*M*y declaration of desire was all it took to break Landon's restraint.

Faster than a cheetah driving a Bugatti, he unhooked my bra, slid it off and dropped it on the ground. Then he whipped off his own shirt, and the dizzying cocktail of Mai Tais and Landon made me lightheaded all over again. He grinned at my obvious awe at his delicious, muscled body, pulled me close and began kissing me again — on my lips, my neck, my clavicle, the upper curve of my breasts.

Before I knew it, he'd lowered me to the sand — well, on top of the shirts, but I was well aware of the sand — and as I lay on my back, he brushed his lips over each nipple, then flicked each hardening peak with his tongue.

"God, yes, more," I said, pushing my breasts up toward his mouth as I caressed his back.

He chuckled, kneading one breast with his hand while he took the other nipple between his lips and sucked hard. Then he tugged at it with his teeth, and I yelped.

"Too much?" he murmured.

"God, no. Hurts so good."

I was sure he was smiling against my breasts as he licked and nipped and sucked some more, because surely those were fireworks shooting through them? I only had a hint of what lovemaking would be like with Landon, and already it was a thousand times better than it had been with that stupid producer and in the couple of brief relationships before him. It was like Landon's mouth was made for me, and oh — ooohhh —

His mouth had moved down to my belly, and his fingers crept to the elastic waistline of my panties, tugging them slowly off my hips. I groaned and lifted my butt so he could slip them off, and then his mouth was on my pussy, his tongue sweeping up my center. A long, low, stuttering sigh escaped me and he hummed in response, the vibrations shooting up through me until I tingled all over.

His invasion was subtle at first — the tip of his tongue on my clit, in my cleft — and then he plunged it inside my wet heat, over and over. Holy sequined crustaceans, how long was his tongue?

And how wet could I get? It was slick down there, almost embarrassingly so, but at least he knew I wanted him.

I wanted him so badly.

He licked and teased my nub without mercy, and then he exchanged his mouth for his fingers, sliding them inside me. I closed my eyes and began to writhe as he pulled and pumped with devastating skill. His calluses fired up an electric friction against my nerve endings as he thumbed my clit while he fingerfucked me. I was already on the edge. As his fingers curled inside me and touched the magic spot while his other hand pinched one breast, I came like a Pegasus with its wings on fire, bucking into his hand. I gasped and held back a scream, moaning "yes, yes, yes!" instead.

I shivered as he withdrew his fingers, and I opened my eyes.

He was breathing hard, too, but he managed a smile, even though his eyes were as serious as a hungry vampire's. "Kayla?"

"Why are your pants still on?" I managed to whisper, and then I grabbed at his jeans, wrestled open the button and tugged on the zipper.

"Ow. Easy. I'm a little sensitive there right now," he said, half-laughing, and he wrenched them off. The tent in his boxer briefs could have held a three-ring circus.

"All off," I ordered, and he grinned and complied, standing quickly so he could slide them off, then lying on his side next to me, on top of his crumpled jeans.

I reached out to touch him. Despite the black night, there was enough ambient light reflected off the clouds for me to see his manhood for what it was: a magnificent erect cock, its dark, rounded head already shiny. I ran my finger over the bead of moisture there and rubbed it into the little slit at the tip.

"Jesus, Kayla." Landon lay back, and I grasped his big shaft and ran my hand up and down its hot, silky steel, slowly at first, then faster. He sighed and lifted his head to watch me. Him watching me touch him was about the sexiest thing ever. Then I couldn't resist. I leaned over and took him in my mouth.

Him watching me suck his cock was even sexier. His gorgeous face betrayed his excitement, his surrender.

The taste of him, salty musk, and his gasps, his groans gave me so much satisfaction. To have this confident guy, this incredibly handsome and capable man, at the mercy of my tongue made me ache to have him inside me.

He must have had the same idea, because after I'd taken him to the back of my throat for a few long, languorous sucks, he gently pushed me away. "Not like this. I want to be—"

"Yes. I want to feel you here," I whispered, lying back, spreading my legs.

"Yeah." He was breathless and fumbled around in the

clothes beneath us, finally pulling out a little square packet. *Shit.* I was glad one of us was thinking clearly. The effects of the alcohol had faded a little, but I was so damn turned on, I was ready to take him raw.

He slipped on the condom and held himself over me, the muscles in his arms taut, his skin rough with sand.

"Touch yourself, Kayla," he whispered, poised over me.

"Get inside me."

"Touch yourself first." His eyes snapped with fire. "I want to see you do it."

Ooo. Dirty Landon. I smiled and touched my already hyper-sensitive bud, making slow circles with my finger as I held his gaze. I let out a soft moan. "I need you to fuck me now, Landon."

He ran his hand up and down his rigid shaft, and he smiled. "With pleasure."

Holding my rapt gaze with his, he positioned himself and eased his thick length partway inside me.

I made a low sound of ecstasy. It felt good. Nothing had ever felt this good. "More. All of you."

"Yes," he hissed. It was like he couldn't hold back anymore, and he pushed hard into me, all the way, his balls slapping against my ass. A pleasurable pain lit like a flame in my core. And then he did it again, then faster, until he was pounding me into the sand, the waves a dim and primeval backdrop to our fucking.

He was big, stretching me. Lighting up every millimeter of skin, every red-blooded cell as he drove into me. I squeezed around him, the tension unraveling as I took him as deep as I could, grasping his muscled arms, drowning in pleasure. My nipples tingled as his chest rubbed against mine.

His shudder against me was like an earthquake. He slammed home as he climaxed, even deeper if that was possible, and exploded inside me.

I cried out and lifted, pushing my pelvis against him, taking him to the end of me, supernova waves of energy blasting through me. Through us. I trembled as I collapsed back against the ground, as he let out a big gale of breath and slowly stilled. He eased out of me, tied off the condom and set it aside, then gathered me in his arms. Skin to skin. Sand to sand.

And then he kissed me again. This kiss wasn't perfunctory. It wasn't a thanks-for-the-drunk-fuck kind of kiss. It was tender, expansive, sweetly deep, sinfully dirty. Open-mouthed and hungry. Understanding and responsive. Fuck, the kiss was almost better than the sex, and the sex was by far the best I'd ever had.

Or ever would have?

What have I done?

"You know, it's after midnight," Landon whispered into my neck when his kiss came to its lazy conclusion. "So maybe this is our date."

"Nacho Day?" I whispered back.

"*Back to the Future* Day. All the days."

I touched his face, drinking in those dark eyes. "Does that mean we can't have a date tomorrow? I mean later today?"

"We absolutely fucking can." He kissed me again.

After another dreamy kiss or ten or a hundred, we came up for air. "I have a feeling I should put clothes on."

"Sobering up?" He chuckled. "You're right. We're lucky no one's out here tonight."

We dressed. He was right. I felt sobriety coming on, and I didn't like it. "Where are my pants again?"

"At the pool."

"Oh, right."

We walked back to the beach house. Along the way, he found a trash can to dispose of the condom. Most of the revelers had disappeared from the pool, though I could hear them inside the house. Damien was still passed out on a lounge chair.

I grabbed a towel from a stack and rubbed as much of the sand off me as I could, then handed it to Landon while I put on my jeans and shoes.

He did the same, left the towel on a chair and shot me the Fireworks. Only now his smile had even more color and light. I was dazzled.

And a little worried.

"Want to head home?" he asked. "I need a shower to get all this sand off."

I nodded, not trusting myself to speak. Imagining a shower with Landon ...

Was that where this was going? More of him? Night and day and night? Or was this just a one-time thing?

But he said we still had a date tomorrow. Er, today.

Today. The VIP party.

Damn reality.

But before then, there was sleep, and before that, there was a shower. I smiled shyly up at him.

He grinned back.

Holy Greek gods, I was in so much trouble.

CHAPTER 23

*F*riday morning, with dim memories of a very thorough shower with my roommate and a deliciously achy feeling in my little-used body parts, I got a call from Millie. Only Millie would be up at 8 a.m. after a night like last night.

I groaned and reached for the phone, noticing that I was alone in my bed. So we'd retreated to our corners. Honestly, I didn't remember much. Except maybe Landon tucking me in. Oh, wait — Landon tucked himself in with me before I slipped into unconsciousness. He must've left already.

"Kayla? Are you there?" The phone was talking.

I shook my head to clear the cobwebs. "Yes?"

"Ticket sales are jumping this morning. The VIP party's sold out."

"Fantastic!"

"Must've been the history radio show."

"But he hates me," I said.

"No publicity is bad publicity." Millie starting going over all her checklists, and I made noises and decisions where appropriate. "Everything's under control. You don't have to rush over there. It's going to be a late night."

"I have some kitchen cleanup to do and stuff," I said. "Thanks for everything, Millie."

"My pleasure. Now I've got to tend to the Bohemia Bartenders' setup. You're going to love the cocktails. Eyeballs are involved." She laughed and disconnected.

Not real eyeballs, presumably. Neil was a purist among mixologists, but I was pretty sure he wasn't a cannibal.

I let myself feel smug for just a minute about Ken Mote-barkle ... and also relieved he wasn't coming to the haunted house, because I was pretty sure it would give him a heart attack. Hell, it practically gave me one.

I slipped out of bed. Oh, wow. I was naked. I never slept naked, not with a roommate roaming the house and having to share a bathroom. Only now my roommate and I had slept together. Naked. And not just sleeping.

Heat rushed through my body as the delicious details of our time on the beach came back to me. I savored each one as I took another shower, this one to wake up, and touched the parts he'd made sing last night. He felt so good. He *was* so good. A really good guy.

Could I let myself enjoy him? Should I expect more? I wanted to expect more, I realized. Maybe I'd been burned by the asshole in Orlando, but Landon had kindled something in me. Hope. Hope was uncomfortable. Hope was scary. But the high of being with him, of thinking about being with him again — it was better than riding a log flume through a dark chocolate river.

I took several deep breaths as I pulled on my work clothes. I was on the ride now. And I didn't see any reason to jump off. Not when I remembered his smile. His smile and everything else. *All the days,* he'd said. I wasn't sure what it meant, but did I mention I had hope?

I checked my email before I left the house and was surprised to find one from my old teacher in Orlando and another from one of the friends I'd emailed about Max Junior's video reel.

"You're not going to believe this, Kayla," my friend Corey wrote, "but that stuff with the hot-air balloons is mine. Who does this guy think he is? I took the liberty of asking a few other friends in a private Facebook group if they recognized the footage, and they were able to attribute three more of the clips to someone else. Watch out for this guy."

My teacher sent a similar note, saying the beach footage had been shot in Fort Lauderdale by a former colleague.

I hadn't given them all the context when I'd sent them the reel, only asked if they'd known Max Kantera Jr. I'd never expected this tsunami of plagiarism.

And now I was in a difficult spot. I wanted to tip off Marla, but I didn't want to look like I was sabotaging Max — my step-brother, even though he didn't seem in a hurry to claim me. Sure, I wanted the job, but this would be a shitty way to get it.

However, I couldn't let this go. Plagiarism was one of the worst crimes on earth, in my opinion. It stole the lifeblood of artists who put their soul into their creations. Everybody online seemed to think they owned everything, but the truth was, they were killing the art by stealing it. I had a lot of friends who were artists. They were having a hard enough time getting by, and if they couldn't make anything off their creations, in the end, they couldn't sustain themselves making them. They didn't need putzes like Max stealing their work.

After much agonizing while munching on a bowl of Chee-rios studded with pieces of banana, I wrote Marla a quick note detailing the theft.

"It's painful for me to write this, and I'm not telling you this to get the job," I concluded, "although I'd love to get the job. I'm telling you this so you don't hire someone who isn't who they say they are, who doesn't have the ethics someone in your office should have. All the best, Kayla."

MILKWEED MANSION WAS quiet and empty when I got there. Almost.

Landon was there, cleaning up the foyer. He wore holey jeans and a white T-shirt that said "Thunderbolt and lightning, very very frightening" with a drawing of Galileo on it.

"Hey," I said, suddenly too tongue-tied to say anything else.

"Hey," Landon said in a warm-butter voice, coming over to me and taking my mouth with his.

Somehow his languid kiss untied my tongue.

"You left early this morning," I managed when we took a breath and stepped apart.

"I saw some stuff on the tour last night I want to take care of. Just a few things here and there."

"Don't clean up all our decay, now. That's the main selling point."

He laughed. "No chance of that. The decor last night really brought out how rough-looking some of those rooms are."

"Don't I know it," I said dryly.

"Are you worried? Tonight is going to be great. I'm feeling really good about this."

"And you should. Because you did everything, Landon. There's no way I could have pulled all this together by myself."

"Oh, you put in plenty of sweat equity." He shot me the Fireworks.

His smile made me want to taste his lips again. I barely

restrained myself. *Take it slow, idiot.* "I wanted to clean up the kitchen a little bit. Just make sure the caterers can use the sink if they need it. Though Millie says they're bringing a truck."

"She's a whirlwind. I think you're in good shape. Great, actually." He scanned my body, my shorts and tight little T-shirt, and my face heated.

I had no idea how I was going to get through this. My emotions were popping like popcorn. Lust. Fear. Like. Deep like. Not the other "L" word. I couldn't articulate that yet, but it was there, just under the surface.

But we managed to keep our hands off each other, mostly, as we did the last-minute jobs to get the house ready for visitors. Landon had an extra portable toilet brought in, so now there were two for guests; only the VIPs and our performers were allowed to use the one in the house, which had been minimally renovated in a retro style under Landon's guidance, with second-hand fixtures.

Separately, we went home to get ready for the night, but he volunteered to drive us both over after we changed into our costumes.

It was almost Halloween. We had to have costumes.

I was a spider woman, dressed in a short, tight, sleeveless black dress printed with sparkly white webs that was a thousand times more daring than my usual garb. It went up to my neck, but it barely came below my ass. My legs were clad in webby black tights, and I wore black flats just in case I had to run from any ghosts. My hair was swept up in a sparkling spider clip to complete the look, and I went dramatic with the makeup. Considering I hardly ever wore makeup, it was definitely dramatic.

Landon visibly did a double-take when he saw me emerge into the living room.

I did the same, because he was dressed in an outlandish two-piece suit. It was black, covered in cartoony white skulls, and had broad black lapels. He wore a red shirt beneath with a black bow tie and his black high-tops. He was ridiculous. Yummy. Ridiculously yummy.

"Where did you get that?"

"Damien hooked me up. Apparently he has a thing for crazy suits."

"It's too bad I don't have the time to undress you," I said, then clapped a hand over my mouth.

Landon's easy, deep voice almost stripped me of its own accord as he walked slowly over to me. "I could make the time."

We had a volcanic stare-off, and then my phone buzzed in my little black purse. I held up a finger, pulled it out and glanced at the screen. "Text from Millie. She says all the ghouls and staff are there and ready to go and where the hell am I?"

"Guess that solves that little problem," he said, his voice a low growl. He leaned in, slipping an arm around me and — hello! — under my short hem to grab my behind, and then he kissed all my lipstick off. "I'm driving," he said when he let go.

"OK," I squeaked. At this point I just wanted to skip the haunted house and fuck his brains out.

Instead, I fixed my lipstick on the ride over, and we made an entrance, since several of the VIPs had already arrived. Tours hadn't started yet, but Ez and the Emeralds were rocking in the ballroom, and the food was making the rounds. Neil and the Bohemia Bartenders were doling out delicious cocktails. One was a variation on the Dark and Stormy with rum and ginger beer, garnished with disgusting-looking eyeballs made from lychees and cherries, and that's the one I opted to try first, carrying it around as I met the well-heeled of Bohemia.

There was a whirlwind of introductions as Alex brought us to a lot of the people he knew from the fundraiser circuit, and they were eager to talk about my plans for an event space. Some of the VIPs were dressed in Halloweeny garb, but most just went with black. It appeared most of the women had taken the advice we'd given them and worn semi-sensible shoes, though there were still a few heels. Hey, some women could run marathons in them, so they'd probably be fine going on the scary tour. Personally, I'd break a leg.

There were a lot of comments on how Landon and I matched and how good we looked together. They were treating us like a couple. It was so weird. I hadn't been in a couple in a while, and to be fair, I still wasn't in one. But this moment of couplehood felt so much better than anything in the past, and I wondered if there was any chance of this feeling in the future.

I was way, way out on a limb on a tree I'd sworn I'd never climb again.

Annabel and Andy, my newfound half-siblings, had shown up, and they were enthusiastic about all the work that had been done with the place. I thanked them for what they'd done — Annabel had made good on her word and sent over professional help a few times in the past few weeks — and I promised I wouldn't be a stranger. They even had a friendly conversation with my mom and grandma, which was totally weird, but their mom wasn't there, saving us all what I suspected would've been a supremely awkward moment.

There was no sign of Max, and when I met Marla and her boss, they said nothing about my little note about his stolen footage. But Marla was super-nice, so at least I'd made a friend, I told myself, even if I didn't get the job.

Landon introduced me to his father, Paul Putter. I could see traces of Landon's good looks in his father's face, though his dad was a lot more sunburned — from construction or golf, I couldn't say. He was friendly and polite, and I caught him giving

Landon a look I found hard to define but wasn't particularly happy with. I think it said, "Yeah, I'd hit that. Way to go, son."

To Landon's credit, he didn't look at all comfortable at the moment.

When Jace made his entrance in his vampire outfit, even the aged ladies among the crowd gasped like schoolgirls and rushed over to meet him. He was incredibly gracious, and I was incredibly grateful.

A striking woman in a vampiric dress trailed him. Her purple-hued sparkling makeup contrasted beautifully with her dark skin. "Wendy?"

"Hey, Kayla!" she came over to greet me and Landon. "Penelope recruited me to be the tour guide after Jace does his thing tonight, so I'll be shadowing the groups as they go through."

"That is soooo cool of you," I gushed. Wendy had been one of the stars of Jace's rewrite of *A Midsummer Night's Dream* at the Chamberlain Theater. I'd heard a lot about it but never had a chance to see it.

"Well, I'm not in any plays right now, and my software job is driving me nuts. I need an outlet, you know?"

"I totally know," I said. "I was recently *relieved* of my job. I guess this is my job now."

She grinned. "You've got your work cut out for you, but this place is amazing."

"Totally worth the effort," Landon said.

"Thanks again!" I said as Jace beckoned for her to follow.

Many of us followed them out to the porch to see the launch of the tours. Jace stood in the yard with the big illuminated wraith billowing behind him. He'd prepared a few words to introduce the haunted house, and he was in the middle of his speech when a car roared up the drive. There weren't supposed to be any cars out here except for some of the people putting on the event, and they'd all parked off to the side to leave plenty of room for guests to stroll around the yard.

The invader was a Porsche SUV, and Max Junior stumbled out of it, holding a bottle and screaming, "WHERE IS THE BASTARD BITCH?"

Then he spotted me on the porch. "Ah. *There* you are!"

CHAPTER 24

"Well, this is awkward," Landon said at my ear, and his droll comment made me do the most inappropriate thing.

I laughed.

"You're laughing at me?" Max screamed. He pitched his booze bottle at me, and the crowd screamed and scattered. I jumped, but the bottle didn't even make it to the porch, just shattered on the walkway.

"I'm not laughing," I said. Now I wasn't, anyway.

"It wasn't enough that you got this — this *house,*" he said, moving closer.

That's when I remembered our security guy didn't start until the next night. I clutched Landon's arm.

"Noooo," Max said, stopping just shy of the porch. Some of the VIPs had gone inside, but others just gawked, unsure whether this was part of the entertainment. "You had to submarine my job, too. What kind of a slut bastard bitch are you?"

"Hey!" Landon said sharply while I gaped.

Marla, of all people, called out. "If anyone killed the job, it was you, sir," she said. "And you know exactly why."

Slightly taken aback, Max wavered on his feet before letting out a roar. "I'll show you what I think of your haunted house!"

He sprinted back to his SUV. I was debating trying to usher everyone inside, not knowing whether he was armed or just drunk, when he revved up the engine, backed up, then gunned it, aiming right for the giant glowing wraith behind Jace.

Jace leapt out of the way with the magnificent grace of Batman swinging from the Batrope.

"Oh, no," I said just as Landon held up his hands and shouted "Stop!"

It was too late. If anything, Max accelerated, and he slammed into the wraith with a loud crunch.

Because the wraith was built atop the giant tree stump.

"Oh, fuck," I said, running out to see if he was OK, followed by Landon, along with Annabel and Andy, who'd seen the whole thing.

"I told you he was drinking again," I heard Annabel say to Andy.

Oh, geez.

The airbags had gone off, but before we even got to the car, Max stumbled out. He was intact, but he had a small, bloody cut on his head, and he seemed as dazed as a zombie. He lurched forward, then fell back on his butt.

Marla had run out, too. "I called 911," she said. "An ambulance will be here any minute."

Even as she spoke, I heard the siren, and a few minutes later, the flashing lights lit up the oaks as it pulled up the drive, followed by a couple of police cars.

Jace called out to his first tour group. "Let me take you to the real show, ladies and gentlemen. I understand you're interested in some haunted real estate?" And by some miracle, he and Wendy got the guests moving as the cops sorted out what happened and the EMTs checked out Max.

"He's refusing transport," one of them told Annabel, who'd stepped up and claimed her brother.

"I'll take him home," she said. "And I'll call a tow truck tomorrow," she said to me.

"No hurry," Landon said, a trace of amusement in his tone. "The car actually looks pretty good there."

It kind of did. The glowing wraith hadn't budged at all. Only now its huge, skeletal claws reached out over the car as if the ghost had caused the disaster.

Annabel also somehow talked the cops out of citing her brother — that's what the reasonable one in a wealthy family did, I imagined — and she came over to say goodbye. Max was now sobbing and saying over and over, "I had an invitation!"

"I'm so sorry about this," Annabel said. "Please don't think any of this is your fault. Someone else on the tourism council had tipped off the chief of the office about one clip in Max's video, but he was reluctant to act because of his relationship with our father. Your letter revealed just how bad it was."

"I'm still sorry," I said, even though Max had tried to take out my wraith and called me some very nasty things.

"He needs some help. Maybe he'll get it this time." Then she hugged me, and they went on their way.

Through it all, Landon was calm and cool, helping out where needed, stepping back when his presence wouldn't have been welcome. And once the Kanteras had left, the party went back to being relaxed and fun, though I heard the buzz around the ballroom about what had happened. I hoped Millie was right about all publicity being good, because this was the kind of gossip that was too good to die here.

I was delighted to see the guests coming back from their tours flushed, excited and laughing about what they'd seen, but not revealing its twists — Jace's parting request to each group was to keep the house's secrets intact. Duncan made an appear-

ance between tours, filming himself in a video blog in his ridiculous spider outfit — he had a zillion followers, so that would be
good publicity, at least. In spite of the evening's chaos, I started
to relax.

As I watched Landon chatting up some of his clients in the
room, that ember of hope in my heart fluttered up into a flame.
This was the day we were supposed to have that "date," his silly
condition for helping me with the house. Our post-midnight
encounter certainly qualified.

And he'd also joked that I'd be in love with him by now. A
familiar fear threw water on my hope, but the heat of the flames
kicked it back.

I was afraid he was right.

But wouldn't it be great to be right? Couldn't it be?

As the tours concluded, Jace posed for pictures with guests.
Millie collected the donations. I said goodbyes and thank-yous
to as many people as I could. As the last few people left the ballroom and the band shut down, I looked around for Landon.

I went over to Neil, our nerdily handsome bartender, who
was packing up the bar. "Have you seen Landon?"

"I think he said something about showing his dad the
garden?"

"OK, thanks." More likely he was showing his dad where
he'd placed the shed he'd donated. I didn't blame him. It was a
really fine shed. I headed to the back door and stepped out.

It was dark out here and fairly quiet now that the band and
the haunters had ceased their racket. But I dimly heard voices
beyond a cluster of oaks and palms. I took a few steps and
stopped when I heard my name.

"Has she agreed yet?" came Paul Putter's voice.

"I don't want to talk about it, Dad." Landon.

"This is the perfect spot. The lot is huge. We don't have to
knock down the house. It could even be a clubhouse. But the

condo buildings will look great on the south end. The river view is fantastic. Don't you agree it'll be perfect?"

"Yes, it'll be perfect," came the offhand response.

"We'll just cut down the oaks ... "

A wave of nausea hit me, and I faltered backward, then turned and ran. I wasn't sure where I was going. I ran around the house and toward the cliff that overlooked the river. I stopped and gasped for breath, my hope crunching underfoot like the leaves.

Silhouetted there against the starry night and the glittering water, the beautiful gazebo promised a future. A future I wasn't going to have with Landon.

CHAPTER 25

I gave Millie my key to lock up, and then I got a ride to Bohemia Beach with Alex and Sloane. They were excited about the big success of the haunted house. Sloane had funny stories about people's reactions to her horrific costume. And I tried to be happy, too, at least until they dropped me off at my mom's.

As soon as she opened the door, I burst into tears.

Here's the thing about my mom. She didn't demand an explanation. She just took me in and gave me a long hug and made me some hot cocoa, loaned me yoga pants and a T-shirt, then gave me a fluffy pillow, sheets and blankets so I could crash on the couch. Nightmares plagued my fitful sleep, but finally I was ready to get up and get on with the day and my new life. Which in one significant way was the same as my old life.

I was alone.

"Have you talked to him, honey?" Mom asked as I drank a cup of coffee at the kitchen table in the morning with her and Grandma Helen. My tummy was too twisted to eat.

"What's there to talk about? He's plotting with his dad to turn Milkweed Mansion into some kind of condo village."

"That doesn't seem like Landon."

"He's a builder, Mom. His dad is a builder. It's what they do."

Grandma snorted. "With a body like that, who cares what he does?"

Mom said, "Ma!" while I said "Grandma!" But Grandma Helen just winked at me from over her coffee cup.

She almost made me smile. "I have a question for you, Mom."

"All right." Mom didn't look thrilled.

"My father obviously knew about me, since he left me the house. Why didn't he try to get in touch?"

"I don't know. I did inform him when I learned I was pregnant, but by then, I'd also learned that he'd lied to me. That he was engaged to someone else. Our time together was brief. Impulsive. We were already estranged when I found out about you. I told him I didn't want anything from him but didn't want to keep you a secret. And he told me he couldn't endanger his future by having anything to do with us. He did offer me some money at the beginning, but I refused."

My poor Mom. She was beautiful still, even with silver strands lightening her red hair. Knowing how badly he'd treated her, how she put her own hopes for love aside to raise me, made me understand her pride in not asking for more, in not pushing him to connect with me. But it still hurt that he never did.

I looked into her clear eyes. There were no tears there now. She was strong, and that was a long time ago.

"I get it," I said. "And you must understand how I feel. You know what it's like to have a guy lie to you."

"I do. And I know something happened in Orlando." She knew way too much. "But before you throw away whatever you have with Landon, be sure you have the whole story. He's a good man, Kayla."

All I could do was nod. I knew what I'd heard.

It wasn't like I'd have to see Landon, anyway. He'd been so absent from his dad's business while helping get the mansion ready for the haunted house, he'd promised to make up for lost work time at Putter Homes. He wasn't even going to be at Milkweed Mansion during the tours.

But that didn't stop him from leaving me several texts.

Where did you go?

Are you OK?

Come on, text me, Kayla. I'm really worried now.

Hey, Alex said they took you to your mom's. Is she OK? Is your grandma OK? Call me.

Kayla? I miss you. Talk to me.

That last one really crunched my nuts. And I didn't have any nuts.

I knew I had to talk to him at some point. I had to disentangle myself from him, disentangle him from the project. Get out of that apartment, though I had no idea where I'd go. Well, maybe one idea, though the thought of living in that gigantic strange house after the fundraiser was over seemed ludicrous.

What options did I have? I didn't have another job. And I didn't have enough money to go into a partnership with an investor if I wanted to retain any kind of control. Control was especially important to me now that I knew what an investor could do with control of the property — an investor like Landon's dad.

When was Landon going to spring the big plan on me? Actually, now that I thought about it, he'd mentioned that his dad was interested in investing. Landon wanted to work me up to it, I guessed. Butter me up, grease the wheels. Get me to commit and then unveil the grand future.

Even as I thought these things, I somehow couldn't believe them. Maybe my man-o-reader was broken, but I just couldn't believe I'd misjudged Landon so badly.

I didn't want to believe it. I wanted to believe in that man who'd made love to me on the beach. Who'd been there for me every day, putting the pieces together. Making everything all right. Because that's what he'd done for me. He'd made everything all right, made me believe that it *could* be all right. Even made me believe that my future would be even better with him in it.

That would be the hardest thing to forgive.

I got some things from the apartment when I knew he wasn't there and crashed on my mom's couch for the rest of the weekend while I worked the haunted house. I took over Millie's role, handling tickets and dealing with details. And it was amazing. Saturday and Sunday were packed, and as the next week rolled in and word got around, ticket sales for the final Thursday to Sunday run exploded.

And still I stayed at my mom's, apologizing for crowding her and grandma in their little bungalow. They actually seemed pretty happy about having me there. But as used as I was to sharing a bathroom, having three women fight over the shower and the sink in the morning was way too much. I knew I couldn't stay there forever, but I wasn't ready to confront Landon yet.

The texts had trailed off, but he still pinged me at least once a day. Did he have no clue?

He's a man, I told myself. *As a rule, men are short on clues.*

After the haunted house, I'd get the rest of my stuff out of the apartment and live in the mansion until I figured out what to do. I didn't think I was cut out for a *Grey Gardens* existence, but hey, I did have a new obsession with roses. And the ghosts would keep me company.

Speaking of ghosts, Penelope told me she'd heard some weird things in the library between tour groups. And she had a psychic streak that I had trouble dismissing.

Could Milkweed Mansion really be haunted? Was poor

sweet Flora still wandering the halls? And was she pissed about our crass entertainment?

Sunday night was bittersweet. The tours were packed — in fact, we went an extra hour to accommodate walk-ups — and it was nearly midnight when the last guests left and we turned off the giant wraith. It was over. I'd bought some wine and pizza, and I sat with the half-costumed ghouls on chairs we'd set up in the ballroom, telling tales and joking around until, pleading exhaustion, they began to gather their things and leave.

"This was really fun," Thea said as I walked her and Duncan, the last stragglers, out to the porch. "I have no idea why I've never tried performing before."

"It's because you're so modest and shy," Duncan said, and I laughed out loud, remembering Thea's screams.

"I usually am," Thea agreed.

"Come on," Duncan said, and then I heard him whisper in her ear, "I know how to make you scream."

I tamped down a surge of jealousy at their easy intimacy. They were chuckling as they walked around the house, out to their car. In the distance, beyond the river and the beach, a flash of light in the sky signaled the end of our dry spell. A low rumble of thunder followed as Thea and Duncan drove out. And then I heard something else.

Another vehicle was coming up the drive.

I took a deep breath of the humid night air as Landon got out of his truck and stood there for a minute, watching me.

He strolled up to the porch, looking more formal than usual, if you can call jeans, a white button-up shirt and a skinny tie formal. I realized with a shock that it was the same outfit he'd worn for the faux dating video.

I looked him up and down, appreciating his look. He was as handsome as ever. And truth was, he still struck a chord in me. My body hummed just having him near, and even my stupid heart tried to beat out of my chest. How could I reconcile the Landon who plotted to turn this place into condo-land with this man I knew, this man in front of me?

Honestly, he looked as uncertain as I felt. "How'd it go?"

I nodded. "Really well. As well as it could have. I don't think we made enough to do what I want to do, but it was great."

Thanks to you.

How could you throw it all away?

He put his hands in his pockets. "I tried to reach you all week."

"I was busy."

"I know, but — I'm sorry I couldn't be out here to help. I owed my dad a lot of time and had to get some things taken care of."

"Yeah, that's what I thought." My voice was brittle. Thunder echoed again across the lagoon as the storm approached from the ocean. The wind hissed through the trees, and I heard the hooting of an owl.

I nodded at his outfit. "You dressed up for clients?"

"No. Family dinner. I wanted to look ... professional for what I had to say to my dad."

"Sounds pretty formal for a family dinner."

"Tonight it was, yeah." He took the few steps up to the porch and stood beside me in the dim light of the faux candle lanterns flanking the door. "Look, Kayla, can we not dance around whatever it is that has you upset? I'm no good at games."

"You're not good at games?" I laughed bitterly. "That's rich."

He took a step closer. Now there was no doubting the worry in his eyes. "Tonight, I told my dad I was leaving the business. Setting up my own company specializing in all the stuff I told you about. Renovation. Vintage homes."

"Starting with this one?"

"What? This will look good on the resume, sure, but — " He

stopped mid-sentence, and his eyes widened. "You heard us talking, didn't you?"

"About the Milkweed condo project? Only I'm sure it will have a different name, won't it? Like 'Chianti Estates' or 'Tuscany Towers.'"

"Holy Christ. You think I wanted anything to do with that? Why do you think I'm leaving my dad's company now?"

For the first time since this conversation started, doubt crept into my mind. "You said it would be perfect. Perfect for cutting down the oak trees and putting up river-view condos and — "

"I was humoring him, that's all. Maybe you didn't hear the sarcasm. I'm not sure how much you heard, because I told him that night there was no way in hell I would help him get into this place, let him work with you."

"You did?" Tears were starting to well in my eyes.

"Yes, Kayla." He grabbed my hands. "This place is special. You're special. There's no way I'm going to let anyone take it away from you."

I yanked my hands from his and ran into the house.

CHAPTER 26

"*K*ayla!" Landon was right behind me as I ran inside the dim foyer. Thunder and a gust of wind rattled the antique windowpanes.

Only it wasn't just the windowpanes rattling.

I froze. Landon screeched to a halt next to me. "Kayla? Did you hear what I said?"

I just stood there, listening. There it was again — not just the house sighing, but that strange tinkling, like laughter, only more melancholy. And then an eerie shriek — or creak. I shivered.

He stepped in front of me, put his hands on my shoulders and gave me a little shake. I looked into his eyes. They glimmered with chandelier reflections.

"What is it?" he asked.

"I think it's the ghost."

He cocked his head, a half smile playing on his lips. "Can we stick to the subject at hand?"

"I believe you." I answered his half smile with one of my own. "I know now you didn't try to sell this place out from under me. I just — oh, Landon, I couldn't believe it even then, but *I heard you say it*. I'm sorry I doubted you."

His smile broadened. "It's OK. Just — talk to me next time, all right?"

"I will." I looked around as a sigh shivered through the house. "Also, I'm not kidding about the ghost."

"Maybe it's the props from the haunted house. There's all kinds of weird stuff in here right now."

"It's all turned off. Do you hear anything else?"

Creeeeeaaak!

A chill shot down my spine.

"Fuck," I said, just as he said, "Shit."

The wind was getting stronger, and another rumble of thunder shuddered through the house.

I had a hunch. Or maybe it was a ghostly compulsion. Almost as if I was being drawn there by an unseen hand, I headed for the dimly lit corridor beyond the stairs and made my way to the library.

Landon caught up with me at the door, which was a lot more cooperative now. It was amazing what oiling and frequent use could accomplish. He gave me a funny look, and then he pushed it open.

The fake candelabras were still on, and the teetering stacks of books were on their sides, deactivated. There was nothing particularly spooky about the room.

Except ... that sound!

It was the creak, the sigh, the tinkling. And an old sconce on the wall, one the electrician hadn't gotten to, flickered.

"Did you see that?" I asked Landon.

"Oh, I saw it."

I looked around at the bookshelves, the grand windows, the beautiful fireplace. The library table and the strange, old furniture. The hidden closet.

We exchanged a look.

"Why would someone lock up a hidden closet and only put a

few old ledgers in it?" I asked Landon. It was the question I'd been chewing on ever since we found it.

"Because it wasn't just hiding old books." He sounded excited now, and Landon hardly ever sounded excited.

Lightning flashed outside the windows, and thunder crashed on its heels. The storm was closer. The wind gusted again, and the noises returned.

I fumbled in my pocket for my keychain, where the skeleton key still hung. Landon threw his tie on the library table, unbuttoned a few buttons, rolled up his sleeves and pushed back the secret wall panel.

"We need a light," I said as I turned the key in the lock of the inner door, my hands shaking, I was so nervous.

"I have my phone. It'll have to do." Landon flicked on his phone's little white light.

I pushed the inner door open. "Look up top, since I can't see up there. I'll look down here."

While Landon felt around on the shelf, I checked the corners again, seeing nothing obvious, just the rough, old boards that made up the walls.

But then there was ... a breath.

A breath of air, and it came *through* the wall.

"Landon!"

"Did you find something?" He bent over to my level, shooting the light into my eyes.

"Damn it, don't blind me!" I waved the beam away.

"Sorry." He shone it around the walls instead. "What is it?"

"I felt something. Like a breeze. Like air coming through the wall."

"Where?" He sounded excited again.

Together, we looked around where I'd felt the strange breath of air. Landon pressed on the boards. I eyed the floorboards.

"I don't see anything," I said. "Oh, this is so frustrating. And it's not even that well-built. Look, a big old square-headed nail is sticking out here. I almost caught my shirt on it." It wasn't much of a shirt, but it was a dressy tank top I liked.

"Maybe you should take it off."

"Funny." And I giggled. Because it *was* funny, and Landon was back, and even if we weren't finding anything, I was happy he was here.

"Where did you say that nail was?"

"Here." I pointed. It was halfway up the wall between the floor and the shelf.

"Could it be that easy?" he murmured. He grasped the nail and pulled.

There was a click, and a small panel about three inches square popped out of the wall at an angle.

"Well, I'll be damned," I said.

He ran a finger along the edge of the panel. "Looks like a handle."

"To a door? To a secret room? OMG OMG OMG!"

"Easy, tiger." He felt inside of it. "It's hollowed out. I'm sure it's a handle. Want to do the honors?"

I hesitated and whispered, "But what if there really is a ghost?"

"Then she probably doesn't use doors."

"Good point." I took a deep breath, hooked my fingers on the handle and pulled.

CHAPTER 27

To my surprise, a door did emerge. It was a short folding door. A corner of the closet folded in on itself and then pushed aside, once I figured out how to manipulate the handle. We'd opened the portal to a dark, musty space.

Lightning flashed, and strangely, it also flashed inside that space beyond, revealing a small room almost overflowing with — it was hard to tell.

But it was creaking and groaning.

"Go ahead," I said. "You have the light."

Landon grinned at my timidity, ducked and went through the door. I followed. And then we were standing in a narrow room, perhaps six feet by twelve feet, lined with tool racks, shelves, work tables, junk and what I could only describe as gizmos.

The chaotic clusters of stuff were made more eerie by the occasional flash of lightning from a high horizontal window that was much wider than it was tall, much like room itself. How I hadn't noticed the window from outside the house, I had no idea. I must've been so busy looking at the inside of the house, I didn't even think about it.

I jumped as the creaking sound we'd heard earlier manifested itself right next to me.

"Is it a machine?" Landon asked, peering at the dark metal thing. It consisted of rings within rings on a stand, only there were cups and other pieces of metal to catch the wind and make it spin. And creak.

"A sculpture, I think. Look, there's more of them. Where's the wind coming from?" And then I realized a very old oscillating fan was operating just beyond the sculptures, churning the contraptions slowly whenever the fan rotated in their direction. "Wait. So that's an electric fan?"

And then I heard the tinkling sound. In the dimness, hanging from shelves above the work benches, I saw wind chimes of varying descriptions — metal, glass, some pretty, some funky and made of bits of junk or wood. And they, too, moved and clinked and chuckled when the fan deigned to blow in their direction.

"But we heard all these noises before the electricity was even turned on," Landon said.

Even weirder, I realized Landon's phone wasn't the only thing lighting the room. From a simple bronze fixture in one wall of the cozy room, a bulb cast a low, orange-yellow light. "But how can there be a modern Edison bulb in here when no one knew about this room?"

Landon snorted. "It's not a modern Edison bulb. It's vintage."

"Vintage? A light bulb can't last a hundred years!"

"Actually, there are a few that have. It's not getting much use. And if it had the special touch of whoever built all this other stuff, who knows."

"It had to have been Stanford," I said. "Flora wrote about him spending time in his workshop, inventing things. But how did all this stuff work and make all those weird noises before we turned the power on?" If disembodied electricity wasn't ghostly, I didn't know what was.

"Remember that flash of light we saw upstairs in the hallway when we first toured the house — a flickering sconce, maybe? And the wires the electrician said went nowhere?" Landon's eyes flashed in another flare of lightning. "Maybe they did go somewhere."

"So there's an independent source of power? Something was generating enough electricity to power this little steampunk nest down here?"

We looked at each other, and then the answer came to me. "The roof."

"All those weathervanes — "

"Are not just weathervanes." I laughed in delight. "And they're powered by the wind."

"And right now, it's definitely windy!"

"I want to see them working."

Landon's grin was otherworldly in the weird light. "Let's do it."

It was crazy to go out in the storm. But I was feeling crazy.

Once we got out into the yard, Landon grabbed my hand. We ran for the gazebo as the wind kicked up to a roar, lightning arced over the house and a tumbling roll of thunder heralded the start of the downpour.

By the time we got to the gazebo, we were soaked.

"You know lightning can kill us even under this roof, right?" I asked him as a wildly forked bolt crawled across the sky and thunder crashed.

"Maybe," he said. "But the finial is also a lightning rod. I added lightning protection that should divert the charge away from the gazebo, and — "

I threw my arms around his neck and smashed my lips into his. He grunted and pulled me close. I licked at his lips, then slipped my tongue inside his mouth, tangling it with his. I reached for his buttons, popping open his shirt as I sucked on his tongue. Then I slid my hands up his hard, wet chest, then around his back, then over his tight ass through his jeans. He moaned and doubled down on the kiss, cupping my behind, lifting me, squeezing me tightly against him as I wrapped my legs around his waist and my arms around his neck and his mouth moved hungrily over mine.

Rain was blowing sideways now, right through the supports of the gazebo, and we were dripping, but I didn't care. Landon had come back to me. He'd never really left. And maybe it was way too soon to think about, but I had a little flash-forward in the wishing well in my brain that whispered that one of the weddings in this gazebo could be ours.

When he set me down, we both had Fireworks smiles. Lightning split the sky again, and I looked up toward Milkweed Mansion. The thunder rattled the world, and in the next flash, we could clearly see the funky weathervanes spinning. A couple of them were quite substantial — turbines, not weathervanes.

I leaned against Landon, and he put an arm around me as we stood there and watched the storm. The rain eased slightly, became more vertical than horizontal, giving us a break in the shelter of the gazebo. It's not like we could get any wetter, but I wasn't inclined to go back to the house just yet.

I nestled closer to him. "I think I know who the ghost is."

"But there isn't one, is there?"

"Oh, I think there is. Or was. It was Stanford Fountain, tinkering away in that workshop all alone, trying to work through his grief after Flora died."

"I think we should check it out in daylight. There was some interesting stuff in there I want to look at more closely. But why did he keep it secret?"

"It wasn't always secret. Flora mentioned him working and

inventing and the servants thinking they were crazy. But maybe he closed it up after she died and made it secret then so no one could disturb him. Eventually, everyone forgot it was even there, and when he died, he took the secret with him. What an amazing person he must have been, creating those wind sculptures, powering parts of the house with his ingenuity."

Landon hugged me again, and then he grabbed my hand. "Ready?"

"For anything."

We took off running into the deluge, across the lawn, back to the house. He left me on the porch for a moment while he grabbed a couple of towels out of his truck, and once we were inside the foyer, he locked the door behind us. "We should get out of these wet clothes."

I raised an eyebrow. "Not that I don't love the idea, but we don't have a bed here yet, unless you count that creepy child thing Damien invented."

"Wasn't there a chaise lounge in the tower?"

I answered his mischievous smile with one of my own. We climbed the stairs to the second floor, then the spiral stairs to the tower. It was really dark up here, but Landon used his phone light to find the blacklight Thea and Duncan had been using for their spider's lair. He switched it on, and the white paper cutouts and streamers lit up in a dazzling bluish-purple glow, reflecting in the windows. So did Landon's soaking shirt, which he doffed and dropped on the floor.

We stared at each other for a fraught moment as rain lashed against the windows and lightning strobed outside. The whole house seemed to respond to the thunder, creaking and sighing, supercharging my heartbeat as I drank in the sight of wet, shirtless, gorgeous Landon. I almost swooned as I had a Mr. Darcy flashback. Maybe Landon hadn't gone swimming in a pond on his English estate, but it didn't matter. *Damn,* he was fine. Even in haunted lighting.

Then it was a race to undress. We watched each other make a hasty attempt to dry off, and I don't know about him, but I really wanted to be his towel as it caressed those muscled arms, that strong back, his taut tummy, those legs, that jutting cock, all while he stared at me with delicious intensity.

He tossed his towel aside and lay back against the chaise as if he'd always lounged on Victorian furniture. Then he shot me the Fireworks and crooked a finger at me.

I licked my lips. "I don't know if I should come to a spider in his web."

"You'll come if you want to come," he joked.

"I think I'm about to come right now."

He laughed, and I moved closer, till he grabbed me by the hand and pulled me on top of him. I straddled him, just south of his hard length, and leaned in for a long, deep kiss.

He spoke softly when we took a breath. "Not to get technical, but I've been tested and haven't been with anyone in a while."

"You haven't?"

"Not since you moved in, anyway. I — haven't wanted to."

Now that was interesting. And maybe just a little bit thrilling. "Really?"

A corner of his mouth turned up. "You're all I've wanted since you answered my roommate ad."

"Get out! In fact you did get out, over and over — you were never home. I thought you were out getting laid. You kept talking about your dates."

"I *implied* I had dates. A man has his pride. It was torture to be home with you when you ignored me."

"Ouch. I'm sorry." And maybe I had ignored him. Maybe I'd been so obsessed with my unhappiness that I hadn't seen happiness waiting for me, right in front of me.

"It's OK. You're here now. And as I was saying ... " He ran his hands down my shoulders, then up my waist, skimming my breasts, making me suck in a breath.

"I'm clean, too," I eked out, "and I never went off the pill."

"So we don't need to put a sock on it?"

"I don't think socks are very effective."

He gave my ass a light little smack, and I yelped, then grinned. Then slowly rubbed myself up and down his cock.

He groaned and somehow looked delighted at the same time. "Do you like being naughty?" he asked in low, mischievous voice.

"I haven't had much of a chance in Loserville, but bring it on, big boy."

He laughed again. "You vixen. This is going to be fun." He slid a hand between us and flicked my clit.

I gasped, then ground against him again. "More."

"So much more." His voice was hoarser now. He slid two fingers in my slippery slit. "Fuck, you're wet."

"We have some towels."

"Oh, I have something much better." He was moving those fingers now, the dirtiest finger-painting ever, and I let my head fall back as I moved against his hand. When I heard about men being good with their hands, I never had anything quite like Landon's dexterous digits in mind.

His other hand slipped behind me, brushing my crease, teasing me, and then he gripped a buttock as his fingers became more frenzied inside me, as his thumb teased my clit.

"God, Landon, I need you — need you to be inside me." My voice was something I'd never heard come out of me before, half groan, half whisper.

"Yes, baby." And his fingers were gone and he lifted me, centering me over him.

I slid down onto his thick shaft and gasped at his hot, hard, exquisite invasion of my body. It was so good without the condom. *He* was so good. And I felt so free with him, weirdly so. Was that because we were friends before we were lovers? We fit in more ways than I ever thought possible. I put my hands on his chest, squeezing, letting my breasts swing above his face. He pulled each breast to his mouth, sucking, tonguing the hard peaks. Then I pinched his nipples as I moved up and down on his cock. His long, low growl was the most erotic thing I'd ever heard.

Lightning flashed outside, its light strobing through the tower, and thunder crashed around us again. Or maybe it was my heart kicking up another notch. He shifted, and I took him deeper. The angle brought the friction of our bodies to my clit, setting the bundle of nerves afire as we slid against each other, faster, faster.

He slipped a hand between us and tweaked my sensitive nub.

The orgasm burst up and out and crashed through me, a rogue wave of pleasure, and it wouldn't stop as he pumped harder, pushing up into me, demanding my ecstasy. I cried out again as he shattered inside me, shooting his seed into me in rocketing pulses. I clenched around him, squeezing him until he collapsed back against the lounge with a gasp.

I fell in slow motion against him, licking his chest, his nipples, kissing his neck and finally his mouth. He wrapped his arms around me, caressing my back, making love to my mouth with his, until our kisses finally stopped and we lay there together in the strange purple light, body to body, heart to heart.

The storm had faded, its thunder now distant. Soft rain pattered against the windows.

"It's after midnight, isn't it?" I murmured.

"Yeah," he whispered, kissing me one more time. "Happy Halloween, Kayla."

CHAPTER 28

*O*ur clothes weren't much drier by morning, but we put them on anyway and headed back to our apartment to shower and change.

Dirty showers with Landon were definitely ruining me for boring clean ones.

We had a lot to talk about, but first we had to clean up the haunted house. *We.* He was going to help me, he said. He was at my disposal, he said. And I was the boss.

Our friends would be coming over to clear out their theatrical accoutrements after noon, but Landon and I wanted to get one more look at the secret room before they arrived.

First we walked around the house and determined that it abutted the west wall on the north end. And sure enough, the siding was seamed there.

"There was probably an outside door at one time," Landon said.

"And look up there — that's the window." I pointed to the long, narrow pane of colored glass set between lines of gingerbread trim around the middle of the house. It wasn't obvious at all.

We'd left the inner closet door ajar so we wouldn't have to hunt for the handle this time. The workshop looked different in daylight. For one thing, the weather was still, so none of the wind-powered gadgets — the fan, the light bulb — were operating. And the window, with its colored glass panels in pale yellow and blue, eerily evoked a sacred space in spite of the informal furnishings — the workbenches, shelves and a tall stool.

While everything was dusty, the shelves also looked neater in daylight. There was a method to Stanford's madness, it seemed. I was spinning parts of the biggest kinetic sculpture, making it creak and groan, trying to figure out how it worked, when I realized Landon had been staring at the same shelf for five minutes.

"What are you looking at?" I asked. "It's not the key to another secret room, is it?"

He emerged from his daze and looked at me. "It's tools."

"I can see that."

"No, I mean these are *tools*. Amazing tools. Rare tools." He had a dazed smile on his face. Not Fireworks. More like beatific sunshine.

My heart beat faster. "Rare?"

"Very."

"Valuable?"

His smile broadened as he focused on me. "Oh, yeah."

"Tell me more."

"Old Stanford must have been a collector. A lot of these he wouldn't even have used in his day — this plane, for instance, dates from the 1700s."

Landon never ceased to surprise me. "How do you know all of this?"

He looked adorably bashful for a moment. "I have an *Antiques Roadshow* habit, and they did a feature on antique tools.

I kind of got into it and did some research, just in case I stumble across one at a yard sale."

"Everybody needs a hobby."

He smirked. "So you don't care how much it's worth, then?"

What a tease. "Landon, darling." I moved closer to him and pressed a light, lingering kiss against his neck, promising so much more. "Please tell me how much it's worth."

"About thirty thousand dollars."

I froze in his personal space, looking into his eyes in shock.

"Thirty — thirty — "

"Thirty thousand dollars," he said, looking pleased. "It depends on the auction, of course."

I swallowed and gestured to the cluttered workbench. "What about these others?"

"They're not all worth that much, but you have a tidy little fortune here." He started pointing them out. "Beveling plane, nine thousand. Thomas Norris English jointer plane, twelve thousand. Nicholson molding plane, five thousand. That bronze pattern-maker plane is worth about twenty thousand dollars. There's a cabinetmaker's plane that's from around Stanford's time that's worth about eighteen thousand now."

"Holy clams on a carousel."

"This is really an amazing collection ... " Landon kept rattling off tool names. I tried to keep track of the values in my head. He kept saying "on a good day at auction," but all told, if we had a good day at auction, these tools together could be worth more than two hundred thousand dollars.

Two ... hundred ... thousand ... dollars.

I gripped his arms just to avoid falling down. And then I kissed him like I meant it. Because I did.

～

AFTER A LONG DAY de-Halloweening the house and thanking our friends again for all their talent and hard work, we ended up back in the foyer.

"It's naked," I said.

"You want to get naked?"

"What? No. I mean, yes, but that's not what I said." I waved my hand around. "The house is naked, and I have a lot of work to do."

"*We* have a lot of work to do, if you'll have me."

I eyed him uncertainly. "But why, Landon?"

He smiled and moved closer, wrapping me in his arms. "Honey, I didn't do all that work for a credit on my resume. I did it for you."

"You did?" I whispered, looking into those dark, sparking eyes.

"I did." He kissed me. "I can't believe we're here. I can't believe I'm here with you. For months I've been waiting for you to notice me. To make a connection. But you were — "

He shut up, but I knew what he meant. "I was locked up behind my wall. I know. And I assumed the worst about you, over and over. I'm sorry."

"As long as you think the best of me now."

"I do." I kissed him. "But you said you're going to start a new company. Have you thought it through?"

"I've thought about a lot of things, but I want to run them by you. The downstairs here is perfect for an event space. We can reserve a couple of the rooms upstairs for changing rooms for events and the like. But there are more bedrooms. I could take one or two of them and use them as offices. And the master bedroom ... "

He gave me a significant look.

"Go on," I said, hoping he was going to say what he was going to say.

"It would be a great place for us to live. Together. I'll pay you rent if you want."

I laughed out loud, and he looked worried. "Oh, gosh, I'm sorry, but I'm not laughing at you. I'm not charging you rent. Not if you're saying … saying you want to live with me."

"In the living-in-sin sense, yes, absolutely, I want to live with you. But I *will* pay my share." He grinned, and the Fireworks went off everywhere, in his eyes, in my soul. "How does that sound? Do you want to live together? For real this time?"

"Yes. Yes, please. Can we keep the tower for ourselves?"

"Of course," he said. "It's your house."

"About that. Once we auction off the tools, I should have enough money to feel comfortable about maintaining control of the business, so I talked to Alex for a few minutes today about him investing in the project. He's totally on board."

"Excellent!" This time Landon kissed me, and I got lost in his mouth, his touch, before he pulled away.

"I have one more thing I want to show you," he said. "Before I spray-painted the plywood on the front door, I checked to see how solid it was, and one of the pieces fell off."

"There's a shock."

He chuckled. "Yeah, well, before I put it back, I got a look at the door. I think you might be interested."

"I didn't think this place had any more surprises," I said as Landon produced a hammer from a nearby toolbox and began carefully removing the plywood from the door.

"It's a shame about these nail holes in this nice carved door, but we'll fix it up. This is the real centerpiece. Close your eyes for a minute."

"Really?"

"Yes, really."

So I did. I closed my eyes for a few minutes while listening to him pry off the wood on the back and front of the door, while noting every creak and whisper of this enchanted haunted house.

"OK," he said. "You can look."

I opened my eyes. And then I opened them wider. The centerpiece of the front door was a stunning stained-glass window. It featured a coy peacock sitting on a branch, in gorgeous blue and turquoise colors, with little crystals inset into the tail feathers that spread out below. A golden trellis with gemlike green leaves and red flowers framed the peacock, with a cloud-dotted, translucent, light-blue sky as the backdrop.

"It's — " I couldn't find the words.

"Beautiful," he said simply. "Just like you."

"I love you," I blurted out. I'd never said that before to a man. And Landon would be the only man I'd ever want to say it to.

He dropped his hammer, pulled me close and kissed me again. When he paused, he pushed back my hair and gave me a new smile, all light and heat and something else. It wasn't the Fireworks. I needed a new name for it. Because it felt like home.

Maybe the Hearthfire?

"I love you, too, Kayla."

CHAPTER 29

$\mathcal{B}$y Thanksgiving, I had a lot to be thankful for. A lot *more* to be thankful for.

Marla called to offer me the video job with the tourism office, and I took it. Maybe I had two jobs now, but they were both dream jobs. And one of them, I was doing with Landon — fixing up Milkweed Mansion.

Or maybe I had two jobs and a passion, because I'd also started writing a screenplay about the Fountain family and the house. If I could raise funds for the house, maybe I could raise money for an indie film, too.

My mom, who'd worked with a lot of nonprofits, hinted that she'd be a great event manager for the mansion. I couldn't have agreed more. So she was already lining up events for the new year as we focused on getting key rooms ready.

And even though our master bedroom suite still needed a lot of work, we'd just made it habitable enough to move in. Mornings looking over the river from our balcony were wonderful ... and second only to the nights.

Though I still had Flora's diary, I'd presented the Fountain family ledgers to the historical society, and Ken Motebarkle had gone on his radio show and announced that he was pleased with how the renovation of Milkweed Mansion was going. I greeted this broadcast with hard eye-rolls. He would likely freak out when he found out the auction of the tool stash was in the works, but for now, at least, I had one less enemy.

Speaking of which, Max Junior had just written me a short note of apology for his attack on our Halloween wraith. He skipped Thanksgiving dinner, but at least we were on the right track.

Oh, yeah. Thanksgiving dinner.

The Milkweed Mansion dining room cleaned up nicely. The kitchen was still in progress, so we brought in most of the food, but we had a most interesting mix of diners for the holiday: Landon, my mom and grandma, Aunt Ginny and Jay, Gary and Ez, and Annabelle and Andy and their mother, Liza. That Liza and my mother got along so well was a bit of a shock, but I just figured it was the magic of Milkweed Mansion at work.

When the delicious early dinner was over, our guests went out to the grounds to enjoy the sunset and stroll among the oaks, palms and recovering garden. A couple of the roses were blooming, and their scent tinged the air with a soft reminder of Flora's plantings.

"Too bad your parents couldn't make it," I commented to Landon as we sat in the swing he'd hung from one of the trees. We had an expansive view of the house, the gazebo and the river from here.

He slipped an arm around my shoulders and pushed off with his feet so we swung gently. "They like cruising on holidays. And maybe it's just as well. I've had a hard time convincing my dad that Tuscany Towers was not going to happen."

I laughed. "Would you really have called it that?"

"It's catchy. If you'd said that to him, I have no doubt there'd be a project right now with that name, complete with a clay tile roof and Italianate trim in carved foam."

"More work for Gary."

"True."

"They seem happy." I nodded at Gary and Ez, who'd gotten out guitars and were sitting on chairs in the gazebo, strumming and singing a tune.

"Are you happy?"

I looked up at Landon. "Do you have to ask? Is the constant grin on my face not enough for you?"

He smiled the Hearthfire smile. "That's good. Because I plan to make you even happier."

"The happiest woman on Earth?"

"Maybe," he teased.

My tummy did a little flutter. It was too soon to talk about getting married, but I had this wonderful feeling of joyous inevitability when I talked about the future with Landon.

The western sun glinted off the metal roof of the house, and the wind spun its weathervanes and turbines, haunting our beautiful home. Life was sweet with Landon. And the ghosts of Milkweed Mansion were safe with us.

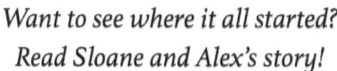

Want to see where it all started?
Read Sloane and Alex's story!

BOHEMIA BEACH
The first *Bohemia Beach* novel
A Golden Quill finalist for best hot romance!

ALEX IS A MYSTERY: **Secretive. Rich. Way too hot for his own good.**

I'm an artist just trying to make it as a potter, and why he wants me, I don't know.

I'm starting over in this beautiful beach town, and saying "yes" to him is part of the adventure. Until *yes* becomes something more.

My new artist friends are quirky and cool. My teacher is alarmingly obnoxious. I'm working hard to get into the big juried exhibition. And I keep losing myself in Alex's arms.

He's insatiable. I'm addicted. But under his quietly forceful exterior is a man wounded to his core.

Can obsession turn into love? And can passion overcome the past?

Or is Alex the worst best thing that ever happened to me?

BOHEMIA BEACH IS a sizzling hot romance featuring an aspiring clay artist, a mysteriously wealthy/seductive/secretly sweet writer, and a colorful beach town brimming with passion, drama and humor. This is the first novel in the Bohemia Beach Series, each a steamy standalone romance set among a circle of artists in the enchanting Florida city they call home.

∼

Learn more at LucyLakestone.com

AFTERWORD

Thanks for reading! Sign up for my newsletter to get fun original content, giveaways, news and cocktail recipes, and I'll send you a free story. I also have a Facebook group where readers can hang out and chat about books and life — please join us in Lucy's Lounge. And you can always find me at LucyLakestone.com!

ACKNOWLEDGMENTS

Bohemia Chills was kind of like a surprise baby, if you'll forgive the metaphor — unexpected but full of joy. I didn't intend another book in the Bohemia Beach Series, but when I heard about the Common Elements Romance Project, this novel manifested in my imagination. Kayla has brief appearances in previous books, and I always wanted to write her story. This was my chance.

Thanks so much to Cora Lee for wrangling the promo for more than seventy authors' books in the project. We all had the freedom to write pretty much anything we wanted as long as the elements were there (a lightning storm, lost keys, a stack of books, a character named Max and a house that may or may not be haunted), but she kept tabs on the titles. Learn more about the other books at https://commonelementsromanceproject.wordpress.com.

Thanks so much to my writing pals Naomi Bellina, Karen Ann Dell, Maria Geraci and Alethea Kontis. This book is partly fueled by coffee and friendship. Shout-out to Spacecoast Authors of Romance: Y'all are awesome.

I'm incredibly grateful to friend and editor Holly Martin,

who had invaluable suggestions after reading this book on a tight deadline.

Thanks also to Mr. Lakestone, who's always supportive of my passions and who doesn't even blink when I stay up until 2 a.m. to write one more chapter.

I'd also like to issue a good-humored apology to lovely local historian Ben Brotemarkle, who is nothing like the historian in my book. It's just that I've always loved his name and thought it would be fun to turn it inside out for a character in my fictional Bohemia.

Though the secrets and architecture of my mansion are entirely invented, there really is a historic riverfront house in Melbourne, Florida, that inspired me. The real house is called Green Gables and isn't quite as grand as Milkweed Manor. A small group of passionate preservationists is trying to save it.

I got Stanford's first name from a recurring name in the Wells family that founded the house. The original owners, William and Nora Wells, wintered there for Nora's health; she lived a long life. And like my fictional Flora, Nora founded the first library in the community. The Wells family also built a high school and a theater. Read more about the house's history and contribute to its preservation at GreenGables.org.

ABOUT THE AUTHOR

Lucy Lakestone is an award-winning author who lives on Florida's east central coast, among the towns that serve as an inspiration for the hot romances of her Bohemia Beach Series, including *Bohemia Beach, Bohemia Light, Bohemia Blues* (winner of the Golden Quill), *Bohemia Heat, Bohemia Nights, Bohemia Bells* and *Bohemia Chills*. She's been a journalist, photographer, editor and video producer but prefers living in her imagination, where the moon is full and the cocktails are divine. She is also the author of a novel of romantic suspense, *Desire on Deadline*.

facebook.com/lucylakestone

twitter.com/lucylakestone

instagram.com/mslucylakestone

amazon.com/Lucy-Lakestone

bookbub.com/authors/lucy-lakestone

goodreads.com/lucylakestone

pinterest.com/lucylakestone

www.ingramcontent.com/pod-product-compliance
Lightning Source LLC
Chambersburg PA
CBHW031952170626
46807CB00006B/2452